biblioteca di letteratura

27

D0393603

RICCARDO ZUCCONI

PAPER HEART

a novel

translated by
Aelmuire Helen Cleary

MAURO PAGLIAI EDITORE

Front cover:
photo by Carlo Cantini

1st Italian edition: March 1998
1st reprint: September 1998
2nd reprint: March 2003
3rd reprint: November 2008
1st Brazilian edition: *Coração de papel*, Editora Record,
Rio de Janeiro, 2004 (tradução de Eliana Aguiar)
2nd Italian edition: October 2013
1st reprint: April 2015
1st English edition: *Paper Heart*, Mauro Pagliai, Firenze,
July 2015 (translation by Aelmuire Helen Cleary)

www.mauropagliai.it

Biblioteca di Letteratura / *nuova serie*

© 2015 EDIZIONI POLISTAMPA
  Via Livorno, 8/32 - 50142 Firenze
  Tel. 055 737871 (15 linee)
  info@polistampa.com - www.leonardolibri.com

ISBN 978-88-564-0318-3

... to my children Corso and Verdiana
to my splendid Lucia

To live our life's the great adventure: fit
For any hero. Nothing else can be
The meaning of our absurd mystery. [...]
We can be sure of death's utility,
Whatever we've accomplished of futility.

R.D. Laing
Life before Death, "Twelve"

The plague accompanied human history for centuries. Recurrent and relentless, it spread terror and death, especially in the cities. There was no art or knowledge that could check its progress and the only defence lay in faith and in the Misericordia. Among the numerous institutions in the world devoted to charity, the venerable Archconfraternity of the Misericordia of Florence is one of the oldest. It derived from the "Società della Fede" founded by St. Peter the Martyr on Ascension Sunday in 1244, for the precise purpose of curbing the plague.

It was originally called the "Società Novella di Santa Maria" and its charitable commitment was to care for prisoners and the sick, as well as providing burial for the poor who died without means or family. The name of the institution derived from its premises in the old church of Santa Maria Novella, where it remained even after the Dominicans built the large new basilica in 1279. Then, in 1321, it moved towards the centre of the city when it acquired premises in Piazza San Giovanni from Baldinuccio Adimari. There, in the shadow of the Duomo of Florence, it was to remain for ever.

I

There are many roads leading to the Piazza del Duomo. Usually Guelfo arrived at the Misericordia approaching the square from Via dello Studio, marvelling at the way Brunelleschi's Cupola would suddenly appear before him, filling the sky between two crooked rooftops. There's nothing to warn you or lead you to imagine that you're about to be confronted by this miracle of architecture and harmony. These are not the predictable perspectives that power has sought in other periods. In Italy in the Middle Ages and the early Renaissance the prodigious and the everyday went hand-in-hand. The extraordinary took place among the common folk, and magnificent buildings were erected between ordinary dwellings. This too was a sign that the people were beginning to wake up, to acquire self-awareness. They funded the building of their own churches, on their doorsteps. This meant that God was closer, and could be applied to without the need for too many intermediaries. That's why the Ghibellines couldn't win.

Guelfo had been captivated by the Duomo since he was a child. Brunelleschi was the true architect of Florence and no-one had left a greater mark on the city. Leonardo and Michelangelo are peerless geniuses, famous the world over. But Florence is the creature of Brunelleschi: the Ospedale degli Innocenti, the churches of Santo Spirito and San Lorenzo, the Pazzi Chapel in Santa Croce, the Pitti Palace and the Cupola.

In the light of a fleeting summer sunset, Guelfo climbed the few steps almost opposite the belltower. Engraved on the marble slabs the letters MVPVM indicated the ancient tombs: P stands for *puerorum*, indicating the tomb of the children, while the others – *mulierum* and *virorum* – referred respectively to women and men. Crowding the steps was the usual throng of Chinese and Russian tourists on organised tours. Guelfo went through the main door into the hall of the Misericordia, greeted the doorman and went down the stairs to the ancient crypt where the two thousand iron lockers of the brothers are now lined up along the walls. He opened his locker, number 1726, and put in the bag holding his basketball kit, sweaty from training. He'd always had a passion for basketball. He'd started when he was a kid, at school, and he'd never stopped since, even though at just over six foot one he wasn't tall enough to be a champion. But he enjoyed it, and it kept him fit. His other passion was *Calcio Storico*, the historical Florentine football that he'd been playing since he was ten years old for the Gonfalone of the Keys in the District of San Giovanni, with the greatest of pride and uninterrupted honour. This was at the time when Gianozzo Pucci was still President of the *Calcio Storico*.

Guelfo's shift started at eight and ended at midnight. He'd been doing it once a month for nine years now. In the first year the new recruits were called *stracciafogli*, after which they progressed to the status of *giornanti*. Before going to take up his station on the first floor, Guelfo looked in to the oratory for a moment. The stunning whites and blues of the large Della Robbia enamelled terracotta altarpiece were still unrivalled after almost six centuries. The splendid Madonna with the Child in her arms was girdled by a choir of angels that looked like newly-opened rosebuds; at the sides stood Saints Cosmas and Damian. The pure light emanating from the relief soothed the soul. Guelfo could never resist this brief visit to the oratory: only in the little Chapel of Vence decorated by Matisse had he ever found anything to rival such light and colours.

Guelfo had almost nodded off when he was stirred by a beep. The control panel showed that 429 had turned off the assigned route. He turned on the microphone and his voice reached the ear of 429.

'You're leaving your area, what's up?'

'There's a block for road works in Piazza Donatello. We have to take a detour by Via Capponi. I'll get back onto my route in Piazza della Libertà.'

Guelfo turned to the computer and saw from the monitor that 429 was telling the truth. The signal went on flashing for two or three minutes and then went off. He was curious, and so he called up 429's record. He always did this: it helped him to pass the time and to understand his job better. He saw that 429 had been sentenced to a year of 2nd level surveillance for not having paid his child support maintenance. He had various previous convictions for insults, threats, drunkenness, poor performance at work and littering public places. Obviously he had no right to vote, although he was fifty-two years old.

This was 2030 and prisons had practically disappeared. Technology enabled complete control of every single individual. The ID card was a microchip implanted under the skin that matched the genetic code and was completely immune to tampering and forgery. The GPS-enabled chip enabled people's movements to be tracked throughout their lives. This made it possible to state with certainty where anyone was at any given time, even many years later. All public buildings shops, restaurants and bars where equipped with alarms that signalled anyone entering without an identity, or with an identity that didn't correspond to their DNA. The penitentiaries were by this stage restricted to just a couple of hundred extremely dangerous individuals on whom, for various reasons, it was impossible to intervene surgically or chemically to prevent their criminal inclinations: the diehards and those who were not compos mentis.

Guelfo looked at the clock and saw that there were still two hours to the end of his shift. It had been a hard day: a full stretch of teaching at the university, then the basketball practice. But he simply had to do this stint at the Misericordia. It was worth lots of points and he was adamant that he would be entitled to vote at the next elections, becoming a citizen to all effects and purposes. Lots of people made fun of him about this: he'd devoted so many days, so many evenings to it, with enormous sacrifices. But the game was worth the candle. He was now thirty-two years old, and the elections would be held again in nine years' time. This time round, if all went according to plan, he would be voting too. And that meant he would be able to stand for public and governmental office. He had lots of ideas, which he frequently discussed with his faculty colleagues in the department. Theirs was the first generation to grow up after the cataclysm that had derailed society. There were great expectations of them: they would not fail.

The last popular elections had been held in Italy in 2013, but by that stage there were elections every year and practically nothing ever changed. The governments were increasingly conditioned by contingencies, terrorised by the daily opinion polls that attributed votes to every single prime ministerial or ministerial move, so that it was impossible to implement a genuine policy of wide-ranging reform.

The European Union, the dream of two generations launched in the 1950s, had been brought to its knees by national and partisan interests. The Nations that had made world history by imposing the Western model and civilisation on all, for better or worse, were now jumping at each other's throats about the price of milk, the fish quotas, and the total reluctance of the various local, political and bureaucratic structures to relinquish any significant share of power. 18% of the electorate turned out to vote, despite the fact that suffrage had been extended to twelve-year-olds, on the grounds that they ought to be the artificers of their own future.

The first election under the new rules was held in 2019. Only citizens aged over forty were allowed to vote. They had to apply for the privilege, after proving themselves worthy by achieving a score of 80% on a scale that took into account their behaviour at work, at home and in society, compliance with fiscal, environmental and ecological obligations and community service. Obviously they also had to have had a clean criminal record for at least ten years. It was a tall order, and most people didn't even bother trying to achieve citizenship. In fact, there were no penalties, and the advantages were debatable, since the commitment and duties of the citizens were much greater than those of the rest of the population. And yet, despite all this, in recent years there had been a great rush to be registered on the electoral roll, which had to be done ten years before the next elections. After this came a whole series of tests and checks which, if you got through them, led to the right to vote and the possibility of standing as candidate. Only 3% of the over-forties had voted in 2019, the first election under the new system. This rose to 8% in 2029. But at this rate, judging by the aspiring voters listed in the electoral roll, in 2039 the percentage would have risen to almost 25%, which was a great result. It meant the democracy that had been beaten, insulted and betrayed by 'free' universal suffrage was coming to birth again and forming a new class of citizens. Citizens who were willing to sacrifice themselves for the common good, to trigger through their work and their efforts a virtuous circle that would complete the change in society.

New York had disappeared in October 2014, destroyed by an atomic bomb exploded in the Trump Tower by a group of Eastern terrorists after two days of frenetic negotiations with the American government. All their conditions had been met, but just when it seemed as though the danger had been forestalled, the bomb was set off just the same. Five million dead and another fifteen struck by the radiation. Along with the Rockefeller Center and the Moma, the Metropolitan and the Plaza, a hundred years of dialectic had gone up in smoke. All that remained of the eternal debate of Western civilisation between individual freedom and the need for State control was turned to ashes.

Within a few months the United States had set up the Confederation, which had been joined by Europe, Canada, Australia, Japan, New Zealand, Latin America and other Asian countries. The rules were strict and primarily related to security. Only inhabitants who abided by the standards established by the Confederation were allowed to circulate, work or trade within its territory. Everyone else was excluded, for good. Being part of the Confederation also meant relinquishing a significant degree of national sovereignty, and compliance with the new political rules established by the United States and the first adherents. The government had been transferred to Hawaii, to the most deserted island of Lanai. It held office for ten years and could not be re-elected. At the beginning there was resistance, especially in Europe, but no one had dared not take the new American political system seriously.

The huge flat-screen TVs that occupied an entire wall of every home, repeated obsessively every four hours, every day, the images of the destruction of New York and its present ruins. The Democratic President of the United States, together with the Republican Vice-President and the government of national unity in permanent session, explained to the world every evening the political and military measures they were adopting. These were then ratified jointly and unanimously by Congress and by the Senate. Democracy is an opening of credit for the *homo sapiens* sufficiently evolved to know how to use it. But if the human race undergoes a process of involution then democracy no longer has a raison d'être and we have to return to decisions made by the few, the wisest, the best. People who take the common good upon themselves in this turbulent and dangerous voyage, carrying to a safe shore the hopes of all in a secure future.

England, as usual, had been the first to offer its support. King William had exhorted his people to submit to the new security measures with patience and a spirit of collaboration.

'We are at war. No-one can deny that, and it is possibly the most dreadful war that we have ever fought because the enemy is within us, in our degeneration. But we can and we shall conquer. England and its King expect that every man and every woman will do their duty.'

The response had been incredible. In 2019 the percentage of voters even under the stringent new rules was 35% and in 2029 it had exceeded 60%. If anything voices were raised requesting that the selection should be made even more rigorous. In England by now people looked askance at those who did not vote. Marriages between voters and non-voters were becoming a thing of the past.

For Italy it had been a hard struggle, and there had been serious opposition and civil unrest. In the end it had reluctantly joined the Confederation, more because otherwise its own economy would have been totally undermined than out of political conviction.

'It was a calamity. A terrible calamity. Imagine that what happened in New York was a huge earthquake. We Italians are accustomed to those, from the time of Pompeii and Herculaneum. But life goes on. Such a catastrophe doesn't mean you have to change world order and rip up all the treaties and agreements.'

But the practical impossibility of selling even a single pair of shoes, a single jumper, just one fridge or a pair of glasses, of welcoming even a single tourist with a strong currency made any such argument irrelevant. And Italy too was forced to toe the line.

The massive computers and satellites that managed the new political system were in the hands of the Confederation technicians. They were all supranational, as were the military chiefs. When the Confederation felt threatened by the behaviour of other States, in either military or ecological terms, it would dictate its conditions. If these weren't met within the set deadline it would use intelligent missiles to destroy a series of increasingly strategic targets, all without using a single soldier. After the first few times, it never happened again. The world was by now split in two, but the number of States applying to join the Confederation continued to grow. Naturally they could only do so on condition that they met the strict standards that were laid down. Only the extremist Islamic world remained obstinately on the other side. But since by this stage energy was derived from water, its importance had become entirely marginal. Alongside the great central power, major centres of local independence were indeed linked to the valleys and the rivers and environmental initiatives on vast scale. The sites of the very first human settlements were swept up in massive projects for the rehabilitation of the seas, the lakes and the rivers, to restore them to their original purity and, with them, the behaviour and the way of life of the inhabitants.

II

It was after midnight when Guelfo left the Misericordia. Casting a final glance at the great Cupola that
watched over the city, he headed off along Via Calza-
iuoli towards Piazza Signoria. By this time most of the
tourists had already left the city centre, and it was possible to walk along the main streets with a certain ease.
Like the Venetians short-cutting along the *calli*, at the
height of the tourist season the Florentines too always
chose the quiet alleys, where you could make rapid
progress just a few yards from the main thoroughfares.

He stopped at Rivoire in Piazza Signoria for a cap-
puccino and a couple of sandwiches. Leaning on the
green marble counter he gazed out at the Loggia dei
Lanzi and the massive pile of Palazzo Vecchio. Guelfo
was a teacher of mediaeval history. He knew the city
like the back of his hand; he knew every inch and every
single day in its history. From its foundation by the
Romans and even earlier, in the Etruscan period, when
Florence had been nothing more than a few ware-
houses and deposits on the bank of the Arno serving
Fiesole above. Not to mention the Pleistocene, when
the whole of the Arno valley was a great lake and the
mammoth roamed the hill up at San Gaggio. Even
now, sandwich in hand, from the door of Rivoire he
surveyed the coats of arms on the facade of Palazzo
Vecchio, beneath the battlemented gallery. Set between
the corbels and the small arches were defensive em-
brasures, from where boiling liquids were poured down
on foolhardy besiegers.

There they are: the nine coats of arms of the Florentine Republic. From left, the red cross on white

ground of the Capitano del Popolo; the red Lily on white ground that was the symbol of the Guelph city; the shield of Florence and Fiesole, half red and half white, the colours of the Republic; the two crossed keys of the Pope; the word *Libertas* set upon a gold ground, emblem of the Signoria; the red eagle of the Guelph party clutching a green dragon between its talons; the coat of arms of the Ghibelline city, a white lily on a red ground; the golden lilies on a blue ground of Charles of Anjou; finally, the coat of arms of Robert of Anjou, striped yellow and black on the left and with gold lilies on the right. Identifying them was a game he had played since he was a boy, captivated by these crests which he imagined fluttering in the wind on the insignia of the Florentine soldiers.

Guelfo stirred and shook himself out of his reveries: he needed to get home fast. Balthazar hadn't been out since five and would be waiting anxiously for him. He traversed the loggia of the Uffizi which had been reopened a few years back, since people had begun to behave in more civilised manner. Up to 2020 the whole of Florence had been barred and gated, which was the only way of protecting it from the vandals. The historic sites and the gardens would be locked at ten o'clock at night and opened again at seven in the morning.

He crossed Ponte Vecchio and turned left. His home was just a few steps away, in Piazza Santa Maria Soprarno. He lived alone. Every so often he would have visitors and, from time to time, a girlfriend. These were colourful affairs: mostly foreigners, colleagues, students, but none of them had lasted more than a month. It wasn't even a conscious decision, that's just the way it went. By now he'd got used to it. And the fact was that Francesca was irreplaceable. He'd done everything he could, but to no avail. It was now seven years since they'd split up. But she was still there, an awkward and stubborn presence, as alive as ever. He'd tried keeping in touch and keeping aloof, seeing her and avoiding her, playing up to her and hating her guts. It didn't make a damn of a difference. She just poked fun at him:

'Guelfo, what phase are we in now? Friends or enemies? Am I a saint or a whore? Can I call you darling?' and she'd laugh down the phone. And he'd always end up laughing too. Laughing at himself, at her, at them, at his ghosts, at his problems. But taking any other girl seriously seemed to be impossible for him. How can you fall in love when you have no further emotional investment to make? When every word, every gesture, every comparison always comes back to the same thing: Francesca, Francesca, Francesca…

He opened the door a little, and Balthazar's enormous black and golden head immediately appeared in the gap. He was a fine six-year-old bullmastiff and he wanted to go out.

'OK, OK. I know I'm late. But let me at least come in and leave my bag, and then we'll go.' It wasn't a big apartment: two bedrooms, two bathrooms, a sitting-room and a little kitchen. Plus a nice terrace, just opposite the Uffizi. It was a fourth floor with no lift. But every single one of the seventy-two steps was fully repaid by this little paradise overlooking the rooftops, with its low ceilings and old terracotta floors. His parents had bought it for him in his third year at university.

'I can't understand why you want to go and live in the Oltrarno, such an inconvenient place. And with no lift, and no garage. But if that's what you want…' His mother hadn't thought it a good idea, but Guelfo was adamant. And so, since money wasn't a problem, the apartment had been duly purchased. He and Francesca had furnished it together. She lived nearby, in Piazza Santo Spirito.

'He didn't have the guts to come right into San Frediano. His nibs stopped at the edge, on the Lungarno!' she mocked him.

'No, no. That's not the reason. It's just that I love this particular apartment. Plus maybe you can leave me just a few yards of independence, or are you jealous?'

'Me? Jealous? And of whom? Of this this beanpole with the forelock, with his athletic build and his actor's good looks, rich, funny and intelligent? Are you joking?'

And they laughed and hugged and bounded gleefully up the stairs, pushing and pulling the last painted cupboard that Francesca had hunted down in one of the local artisan's workshops.

'You just keep quiet. In any case you have no idea at all what it's worth. Just leave the price to me,' she'd say to him, leaving her free to barter and bargain. In any case everyone in the Oltrarno knew her. She'd been born there.

'Franceschina, do whatever you want. Take it, bring it home. Try it. If you like it, you can come back and pay for it. Otherwise you can bring it back.'

'And who says I'd come back to pay for it? And if I didn't come back?' she teased.

'If you don't pay for it, your dad will. Otherwise when I see you passing by I'll grab hold of you by the arm and drag you into the workshop and make you polish furniture until we're quits. And now, be off with you! I haven't got time to waste!'

Balthazar bounded down the stairs, with Guelfo in hot pursuit. 'Don't pee on the footpath, got it?' Within seconds they'd already turned up the Costa. When they got to Porta San Giorgio, Balthazar was happily turning into Via San Leonardo.

'Wait, it's late, we're doing the short walk tonight.' And Guelfo started off down the hill towards San Niccolò, skirting the walls. They came out on the Lungarno and walked as far as Ponte Santa Trinita. Guelfo sat down on the parapet. Florence was spread out either side of the Arno, silent in the summer night. There'd been a heavy storm during the day and finally the air was clear. After many days of sultry heat the city had cast off its shroud and stood out clear against a brilliant black sky.

'You know, Balthazar, she's the reason I stayed. Florence, with these living brown stones, these red roof tiles, these icings of marble. In the brief space of just a few years, they were made and set in place by skilful hands, by the hands of our own people. Something that happened just once in the history of mankind: the final gift of the gods before they disappeared for ever. Anything more is impossible. After that, all we can do is look back. Come on, old chap, let's go home.' Guelfo passed his hand one more time over the stones of the bridge. The bridge destroyed by the Nazis in 1944 and miraculously rebuilt, stone by stone, in a labour that only love could accomplish. He stroked the stones delicately, feeling their warmth as if they were the shoulders of a sleeping woman that you want to wake but don't dare to. The touch brought back a familiar, ancient sensation, along with the memory of when this complicity had begun, this sentimental relationship between him and his city.

When he was a little boy, on Sunday mornings his father would sit him on the crossbar of his bike and take him to visit the museums and churches, to clamber up the hills and wander through the gardens. And they would take the city by surprise, suddenly revealed in a different light, without her knowing, without her seeing them. His father would tell him fabulous tales about incredible adventures. About the Medici crest with the six red balls, which were none other than the prints of the bloody paw that a lion had left on one of their shields before it was killed. About Benvenuto Cellini when he was casting the statue of *Perseus* and, finding the temperature of the kiln too low, set fire to his own house. About Brunelleschi standing at the foot of the scaffolding in the middle of the Duomo, herding the workmen up it at sword-point because they were terrified that the whole thing would collapse.

They couldn't see how that immense structure could support itself on its own. But Messer Filippo, he knew. He had his Cupola crystal-clear in his own mind, and in the end he won.

Guelfo himself had felt something similar, when at the age of six he had walked trembling around the balcony alongside Vasari's frescoes, and he felt even smaller than he was, dwarfed by that magnificent work, as if he himself were a figure in the fresco. A little dark-eyed cupid in his Casentino wool coat with the fur collar.

'Hey, look down, don't be afraid. It's been standing for more than five centuries, it's not going to fall now!' his father reassured him. And so Guelfo had got down on his hands and knees and had poked his head between the iron bars of the railing. Just long enough to cast a very, very quick look at the main aisle of the Duomo, where the midday mass was being celebrated.

'Daddy, I can't do it! It makes me dizzy.' And he had covered the last few metres clinging fast to that strong hand, his eyes tightly closed. He was excited by the smell of the incense that rose from the high altar, and the song that his father was softly whistling, just as if he were at home. This song was the ultimate impertinence of a family of anti-clericalists who, as far back as his Garibaldi-supporting great-great-grandfather had rejected the sacraments.

And this love had gone on growing, slowly and steadily, crystal-clear. A child and his city that cradled him, watched over him and saw him grow. It was since then that he had developed this almost mechanical habit of touching the stones of the walls, of counting them as he walked in the city centre or as he came back from school: first the low ones, then higher and higher up as he grew older. There was no-one who knew that layer of Florence between two-and-a half and five feet as he did. Even now, he always automatically selected the wall side of the footpath, even as he was talking to other people. Then, when he came home, he would notice the dust on his fingertips. And countless times he'd argued with other boys when they wanted to write on the walls with spray paint. 'Here no! Go and daub the walls in the suburbs. These ones no: they're alive!'

Balthazar was merrily chasing a tabby cat through Piazza Frescobaldi. Guelfo had to run after him, his steps echoing as he pursued the dog up the deserted alley called Presto di San Martino. 'Stop, Balthazar, stop! It's getting late.' The tone of his command can't have sounded too convincing, since Balthazar just went on running, faster than before. Within seconds they were skimming past the church of Santo Spirito, and then they emerged in the middle of the square, where the dog suddenly stopped to drink at the fountain. The square was deserted except for two youngsters sitting on a bench deep in conversation. Guelfo shook himself. He had been leaning with outstretched arms on the basin of the fountain to get his breath back. Now he raised his eyes instinctively to where Francesca's windows were. Although he lived only half a kilometre away, Guelfo realised just how much he had been avoiding this place. And yet the piazza was the throbbing heart of the district, with its bars and restaurants, the stalls selling flowers and vegetables, the street vendors, as well as a constant stream of musical events and performances in the evenings.

Since the end of the previous century the Florentines – the last genuine Florentines that is – had withdrawn to the south bank of the city, the Oltrarno. Despite the hardships: the old houses, hardly any of them with lifts, the scarcity of garages, few schools, high prices, lack of services and so forth, the real Florence – what was left of it – was here. The San Frediano folk were the Florentine equivalent of the Yanomami Indians.

Lots of people had gone to live in the suburbs, where living conditions were apparently easier, and because they could no longer stand living on top of each other in the narrow streets of crowded houses. They could no longer stand the constant traffic of human noises and smells in a proximity that had become undesirable the moment it lost the sense of solidarity that had infused it. But such folk were considered traitors who had abandoned their roots and gone astray. They had been replaced by the bright children of the middle-classes, among whom a tacit grapevine was in operation. They bought up the old houses and renovated them and filled them with their lives: lives that, in many cases, had been frittered away or squandered in the past, and in other places. Now they were picking up the scattered pieces along the sides of those streets. Streets where you could find a sense of identity and of belonging, where love – both physical and sentimental – was a palpable presence, almost redeeming the hatred of so many civil wars that had spattered them with blood for centuries. Others had come from further afield: from England and the United States, from Germany and South America, from Japan and Australia. Because being Florentine is a state of mind, an innate sense of grace and proportion. You can be born there and not realise it, until one day, encountering this city, it suddenly dawns on you that it's the only place in the world you can live in.

But Francesca had left. She'd been living in Paris for years now. After graduating in history of art, she had won a UNESCO scholarship and had never returned. Her career was going from strength to strength: she held training and refresher courses for the officials of South-American museums. She only rarely returned to Florence, but she'd kept the apartment, even after the death of her father.

Guelfo sat down on the chipped stone rim of the fountain. He wasn't sleepy any more and his tiredness had passed. He looked at the five windows on the top floor. They were dark, but the shutters were open, folded back against the facade. Francesca didn't want them closed, even if the apartment remained unoccupied for months on end.

'It's not fair that my things have to stay in the dark, never seeing the light of day. It's not their fault that I'm not there.' Francesca had always had a strange habit of anthropomorphising objects, attributing them a soul and feelings. She used to chat with her dolls and her soft toys. She refused to replace her broken-down old bicycle because she was certain that it would have been deeply hurt. She wasn't mad or even schizophrenic. At one point, her father became quite concerned about it. But it was simply a habit. Maybe it was because after her mother had "gone home" (for Francesca, she hadn't left, she had simply gone home), Francesca had been very lonely, and the objects, her things – mummy's things – had kept her company. She spent hours at her mother's dressing-table, brushing her hair with mummy's brushes and using her creams. She only used a tiny amount, so that they would last for ever. And then her mother's perfume was all around, filling the room and touching her every time. Her mother had left everything exactly as it was, to give Francesca the impression that her departure was temporary. Afterwards, no-one had the heart to touch anything. It might seem morbid, but it wasn't. It was her transference, the contact with her soul. Every morning Francesca would get dressed in there, and by now her things were mixed up with her mother's in a single inextricable embrace.

She had talked a lot about it to her father, and they had decided that, at this stage, Laura's presence in their lives was so strong that it could not be erased simply by concealing the signs of it. And then it's not as though Laura was dead. She phoned Francesca frequently and she sent her long letters. Thick sky-blue envelopes full of drawings and ribbons, petals and fragrances which opened like little caskets, spilling their colourful and fabulous contents onto the table. For Francesca, these letters were her diary. She hoarded them jealously. With some she had made collages, gluing the little things found in the envelope onto the pages, along with some cut-out phrases, and then pinning them on the walls of her room.

While he was sunk in these reveries, Guelfo was toying with the key-ring hanging from the belt-loop of his jeans. Two dazzlingly white keys stood out among the six or seven coloured ones. Francesca had given them to him after her father's death.

'Please take them. I'm never here. You never know, if anything comes up...'

'But doesn't the cleaning lady have a set?'

'Yes, of course. But the cleaning lady's the cleaning lady, and you're you. That way it won't be lonely...' A lump had come to her throat. Guelfo had taken the keys. It was no time to make a fuss. The funeral had been just a few days before, and Francesca already had her bag packed, ready to go back to Paris. They were there in the apartment to say goodbye, and because Francesca wanted Guelfo to take anything he wanted that had belonged to Giovanni.

'Please, help me. I don't want to argue. It's a hard time for me. I beg you to accept, you know how fond he was of you.'

And so they had gone down the stairs with a suitcase each: she to go to the station, and he to return home with some jumpers, a few books and some photographs. But he'd never used those keys, even though he insisted on carrying them round with him, almost like an amulet. Except just once, when a pipe had burst and the floor below was being flooded. Francesca had woken him up in the early morning with a phone call, and he had brought along a plumber to repair the pipe.

But tonight pure chance had brought him there, right under her windows, alone in the dead of night... He fitted the key into the lock of the front door and turned it and it opened gently. He began climbing the old stone steps with Balthazar behind him, pushing his head between Guelfo's legs and the wall in an attempt to pass. When they got to the top, Guelfo hesitated for a moment before going in. What if there was someone there? But who on earth could be there? He closed the door behind him and didn't switch on the light. He knew the apartment inside out: he'd been there thousands of times. He'd eaten there, slept there, studied there and made love there. You could say that he'd been born again in that apartment. And yet this evening his impression was different. The light from the streetlamps in the square flooded in through the large windows, mingled with moonlight. The entire room was pregnant with moonlight, and the furnishings seemed to be floating in the void. Bodies and shapes lost in space.

He crossed the sitting-room and the library and went into Francesca's bedroom. By now his eyes had got used to the darkness and he could see well, and the little light there was stirred his memory. In the dark the things lost their colour but began to speak. In the half-light he could picture Francesca better, hear her voice. He was certain that, if he turned on the light, she would vanish along with his memories.

.

III

Guelfo and Francesca had met at primary school, at the convent in Via Laura. As it was a good school and close to home, he'd been there since the first year. Francesca had arrived half-way through the second year, after leaving a school in the Oltrarno where she hadn't been happy. They had become friends and shared all the rituals of early childhood: children's parties, playing in the park, as well as an intense school life every day from half past eight in the morning to half past four in the afternoon.

Francesca was brighter, always better at school, always top of the class: desk in the front row, first prize. You might say she was almost too conscientious, laden with praise and medals. Guelfo was lazy and scraped by: middle of the road. He longed for recreation, when he could let himself go on the football pitch. He explored the big school from top to bottom, trying his best to keep out of the way of the teachers and the nuns.

There was an infinite maze of winding corridors going up and down: long ribbons of yellowish terrazzo flooring, worn by millions of footsteps. Guelfo traversed them sure-footedly, accompanied by two or three other dauntless classmates. Usually they would start in the attics, crammed with chests, old books and registers, costumes from the school plays, even some wigs and a skeleton previously used in the biology classes. They would tap the walls in search of hidden alcoves, concealed treasure. What a laugh – that time they had discovered hundreds of chamber pots, piled on top of each other in tall columns.

'This is where the nuns used to wee, them pissing sisters!!'

And he brought about a dozen of them back to the classroom, where he was greeted by ribald hilarity, swiftly followed by the most unholy scene. He was suspended for three days, and got a good spanking at home. But it had been worth it, and he chuckled to himself at the recollection, still as clear as ever.

Guelfo had a brother, Lorenzo, who was a few years older and was in a higher class in same school. They walked to and from school together, and it was Lorenzo who helped him with his homework and who asked the teachers how he was getting on: the same teachers he'd had himself.

'How's my little brother doing?'

'Fine, Lorenzo, he's doing fine. But he's not like you at all. Guelfo is so fidgety.'

The boys' parents were very busy with work, and they were pleasantly surprised to see how they could rely on Lorenzo to look after Guelfo. He took his little brother everywhere with him, and Guelfo could be seen trotting along at his heels with all the cheerful trust of a wolf cub following the leader of the pack.

One of Guelfo's earliest distinct memories was when a sudden thunderstorm had broken out while they were in Piazza D'Azeglio, and they'd taken shelter under the huge sycamore trees. He could still recall the magical fragrance rising from the wet soil just a few feet from where they were standing: it was like the grateful sigh of the parched earth at the touch of the moisture it had been yearning for. The memory of that smell had remained with him since.

'Come on! Let's go home. The rain's not going to stop and you know that it's dangerous to stand under trees in a thunderstorm. They can be struck by lightning and then we would be burnt to ashes!' said Lorenzo. Guelfo didn't know. He was only six years old, and he didn't even know what catch fire meant. But he had a boundless trust in Lorenzo, who at the age of twelve knew everything and was strong, good and generous. In the square and at school the other boys looked up to him for his integrity. For Guelfo his word was beyond discussion. Very often, rather than playing with boys of his own age, Guelfo would try to join in Lorenzo's games, settling for small "supporting actor" roles. And so he'd stand behind the makeshift goals consisting of schoolbags and would scamper off happily to fetch the balls that went off the pitch. Or he would select stones for the catapult that Lorenzo was so clever with. He preferred to share Lorenzo's world, even as a fifth wheel, than to have one of his own.

He was certain that Lorenzo, when he grew up, would become a great military leader or a general, and that he would be there at his side, his right-hand-man. The only one Lorenzo could trust. And he'd have saved his life a thousand times, in a thousand different ways, deviating the traitor's blade, arriving at the head of reinforcements at the fort under siege and without ammunition, or, best of all, placing himself between his brother and the deadly bullet or arrow aimed at him. Then he would have died in Lorenzo's arms, uttering one last memorable phrase. And his brother would have avenged him, he would have been ruthless with his enemies. Day after day Guelfo discovered the real world, through his brother. Lorenzo, who had a patient and reflective character, would spend hours explaining things to him: from the secrets of Meccano or Lego to how to make a bow or a kite.

Now Lorenzo was gone, he too in a certain sense a victim of the catastrophe that had swept away the system, the old world. In 2014, at the time of the destruction of New York, Lorenzo had been twenty-two. He was studying architecture with the same seriousness that he brought to everything he did. In the difficult years between 2014 and 2015, his faculty had been in the vanguard of the opposition to the new order. Strikes, sit-ins, demonstrations and clashes with the security forces: Lorenzo was in the thick of it. He'd been stopped, arrested and released. He'd given his all without a thought for himself. He saw the whole thing as so absurd that he no longer attached any value to living in the changed world that was coming into being.

'This terrible tragedy will not have been for nothing, after all. If Italy goes it alone, it can reorganise itself on stricter, more ethical grounds. We have to accept that we will all become much poorer so that we can forge a society with strong values, where everyone is equal. We have to return to a survival that is bound to the land, to the community. This is our last chance. This system is the real Tower of Babel, forcing us to constantly step up production. It only takes a drop of one per cent in the gross product for the whole economy to topple, spawning legions of unemployed. Let's leave the Western world and global capitalism to go their own way, and let us rebuild our Nation.'

But the decision had gone the other way and Lorenzo refused to accept it. After he had returned from one of his clandestine meetings, he and Guelfo would have long discussions about it far into the early hours of the morning.

'Guelfo, do you understand? Everything's at stake here: our history, our civilisation, our future. We will become mindless, remotely-controlled robots: subhuman. And that's not to say that I don't agree that things couldn't have gone on the way they were going. It was a total disaster, brought about by the couldn't-careless attitude of overweening egoism, and a complete lack of values and spirituality. Over the years I've made myself sick over it.

And have you ever asked yourself why, in the end, it was New York that went up in smoke? Because it was emblematic of the whole rotten system, taken to extremes. Money, things: the abnormal number of commodities was the cancer that ate away and destroyed the soul of Western civilisation. And Florence has to take its share of the blame for the whole thing. This is where the modern world began: here, where geometrical perspective was introduced into art for the first time. In other words, the way of looking at people as if they were objects, which was to become the germ of the scientific method. It was here that time came to be defined as the private property of man, which in the end brought us to "time is money". From Florence, Paolo Dal Pozzo Toscanelli made a decisive contribution to Colombo's voyage. Another Florentine was the first to grasp that America wasn't the Indies, and the new continent was named after him. Since then, the discovery of America has been the model for the Western approach to knowledge, to science and to the relations with the cosmos. It was here that capitalism took the decisive steps that led it to the conquest of the world.

The only one who sought to oppose it was Savonarola, the disarmed prophet. The city, which reached the height of its splendour just a few years after the death of Lorenzo il Magnifico, was behind him in the quest to unite natural happiness with morality and faith. The pile of wood that they burned Savonarola on in Piazza della Signoria interrupted this attempt, the high point of the Renaissance, and marked the start of the era of Descartes, Newton, Adam Smith and Napoleon, the developments of which were to lead to the catastrophe. But what they're attempting to do now to put things right is intolerable. Total technological control will never work. The cure is far worse than the disease.'

Guelfo agreed. It was unthinkable that on such an important matter he could have an opinion different from that of Lorenzo: 'Yes, you're right. But what can we do about it?'

'I don't know. But we have to do something. There are so many people who feel the same way about it.

Most of the trade unions, important sections of the Catholic Church, and a huge number of intellectuals.'

'But it seems as if the government and parliament have already decided. According to them, we have no choice.'

'That's because they lack courage. And they're imposing their decision on the people, which is a violation. Have you wondered why they didn't accept the referendum that we proposed? Because they're afraid of losing! And that's violence, that's prevarication. It's no longer democracy. But, if imposition it has to be, why haven't they got the courage to make different, more difficult choices, that go in the opposite direction? No they don't want to even attempt that path. We are at a decisive parting of the ways. We have to decide whether to follow the herd or carve out a different path for ourselves: a difficult path, obviously, but a better one.'

'But how can Italy be left on its own, abandoning all the countries with which we've had indissoluble relations for so many centuries?'

'Well, Italy would obviously lose a great deal. But think about it: we would be the most evolved, the most industrialised and the most cultured of the nations left out of the heap. We would inevitably become the benchmark for the entire third world. Our universities would be filled with their students, and their ruling classes would be trained here by us. In this way we could guide them towards this ideal – at once so ancient and so new – the opposite of the other one. It would undoubtedly be a challenge, but a very exciting one.'

Lorenzo would get very worked up and would go on for hours; he was brimming with hopes and plans. But, as was inevitable, things didn't turn out that way. There was a massive campaign in all the mass media, both national and international, promoting the Western solution. Lorenzo's mood had turned gloomy.

Some of his friends had gone into hiding; they'd gone south, where there had been many attacks and an armed resistance was being organised, exploiting the support of the mafia and organised crime racketeers, which were naturally opposed to the new security measures. But Lorenzo found the idea of joining forces with such people repugnant. He stayed at home and hardly ever went out. When his turn came for having the microchip inserted, he didn't turn up. For the moment no sanctions were envisaged, since the system was not yet operating at full tilt. But in practical terms, month after month, it became more and more impossible for him to live. He couldn't enter any building. He couldn't buy anything. He spent hours on end on his PC, communicating with other people – friends and strangers – who felt the same way he did, engaged in a resistance that was both virtual and sterile.

At home, his parents tried in vain to convince him to change his mind. They asked Guelfo to do what he could, because they knew how close the brothers were. However, although he was much less inflexible than Lorenzo, Guelfo felt the same way about things, and he told his parents that the only thing they could do was to leave him in peace.

Then one evening, Lorenzo went out with some friends who had come to pick him up in their car. He never came back. At around four in the morning the doorbell rang: it was the police. Two hours earlier Lorenzo and his friends had driven through a road block on the ring-road avenues. They'd lost control of the car and had crashed into a tree. Lorenzo was killed instantly.

IV

After primary school Guelfo and Francesco had lost touch with each other. He had stayed on at the middle school, while she had gone back to the Oltrarno. They met up again later, when they both went to the Michelangelo secondary school for classical studies in Via della Colonna, which had an excellent reputation.

For Guelfo this school, the "Mickey" as it was affectionately known, was a foregone conclusion. It was just a few yards from his home and he'd passed in front of it thousands of times for as long as he remembered. Mingled with the envy and admiration that he felt for the older kids that he saw milling around in front of it was the certainty that, one day, he would have gone there himself. Guelfo loved that old convent, which was still so austere and somehow decrepit, despite the fact that it had been recently renovated and provided with a lecture hall and a good library. He would walk down the long corridors paved in red terracotta, traversed for one and a half centuries by thousands of students and teachers. He'd started in the first year, at the age of fourteen. He'd crossed the threshold that September morning with the greatest satisfaction. *Hic manebimus optime*, he'd said to himself, immediately exploiting the few scraps of Latin he'd studied over the summer to make a good impression on his new teacher.

Francesca had arrived two years later, in early December of the third year, in the course of her endless peregrinations among the schools of Florence. Guelfo hardly recognised her. Francesca's beauty was something that flowed from within: it was nothing so banal that it had to be measured by the canons of feature or centimetres of flesh. If that had been so, one day she might have lost it. No, her beauty had deep roots: it was internalised and it belonged to her for ever. It was in her every movement, in the tone of her voice, in the ceaseless sparkle of her grey-green eyes, in the highly mobile and open countenance in which you could read all her passion for life and her brave heart. It was in the innate and confident taste with which she chose people, topics of conversation, clothes. It was the beauty of a fearless goodness, which no-one could ever take away from her.

But it had been impossible to resume their old intimacy. Guelfo, after a fairly good first year at the school had teamed up with the wildest and least brilliant bunch. He spent a lot of time larking around, making fun of the girls and playing tricks on them, sometimes quite nasty. Francesca had been unpleasantly surprised by this change. She wondered what had happened to her old playmate, who had been a live wire certainly, but goodhearted with it. She'd tried to discuss it with him a few times, but Guelfo was always surrounded by his friends, in that phase of adolescence when our own characters are still too indefinite and we opt for that of the group. Once Francesca herself was the target of the umpteenth prank. They had kidnapped her during break time, and the nastiest of the bunch, with that infallible nose for these things that youngsters have, had realised that Guelfo was awkward about it, that he wanted to defend her. And so, as the lout held her down with the help of two others, he ordered Guelfo to scrawl something smutty in felt pen on her white shirt. Guelfo snorted and tried to laugh it off; he wanted to leave off, but the others insisted.

'What a big kid you are! You're scared! What's this stuck-up little cow to you?'

And so he'd had to go through with it. Without looking her in the eye, quickly and with a trembling hand Guelfo sketched out a rapid, clumsy doodle. Francesca felt as if she would die. Not at the violence or the insults of those cretins, but at Guelfo's betrayal, his inability to break his bond with the gang, lowering himself to perform a gesture that clearly humiliated him. In those few seconds, the felt pen had become a knife, and the scene fraught with drama for both of them. Francesca felt like Annie Girardot being stabbed in the film *Rocco and his Brothers*, one of her father's favourites that she'd seen at the film club.

'Guelfo, stop! It's me, your friend,' she had yelled with her eyes, 'don't do this. Stand up to them!' But Guelfo had avoided her eyes. After that, they let her go, laughing nervously and running off all together. She had taken off her shirt and put it on inside out; then she'd run home to change and got back to class twenty minutes late. After school, the gang was waiting for her at the gate.

'Francesca, what happened to your nice white shirt? What have you done with it? Are you keeping it for Sunday mass? It would certainly make a killing in church!'

But they weren't threatening. What they really wanted to do was re-establish contact, make her realise that, as far as they were concerned, the whole affair was over and done with. Because the truth of the matter was that they were intimidated by Francesca's intelligence and integrity, by the respect the teachers had for her. But she wasn't going to give them any satisfaction. She replied by laughing and jeering at them. And so, when she'd gone a few yards and was on her own, Guelfo found the courage to go up to her and stop her by putting a hand on her arm.

'Francesca, I'm glad you're not angry. You know, I didn't want...'

She had jerked her arm free roughly and turned two blazing eyes on him as she hissed in his face: 'You are a pathetic coward, you're worthless. I don't care about the others; I hardly even know them. But you! I thought you were my friend! You're nothing to me from now on. Don't ever dare to speak to me again.'

And she'd kept it up. For a year and a half they met practically every day and Francesca would look straight through him. Over time they'd both got used to it, although Guelfo did his best to keep out of her way. Nevertheless, often he spied on her in secret.

After Lorenzo's death Guelfo didn't go back to school for over a week. He was a wreck. The accident had been reported in all the newspapers, and he had the impression that everyone was staring at him. His friends gathered round to console him.

'We've been trying to track you down over the last few days, but there was never anyone at home.'

'We were in the country with my grandparents. My parents wanted to be on their own.'

Francesca too had come forward, along with the others. After all this time she had finally looked him in the eyes again. 'Guelfo, I'm really sorry. Tell your parents too. I've always had such good memories of Lorenzo, of when we were kids and he'd play with us. He was such a good lad. I can't believe it.' And then she'd solemnly shaken his hand, as if to endorse a new pact, to mark the end of a bad time. He'd murmured a thank you and had moved away to his desk, still too shocked by the whole thing, and just wanting to be on his own and far away.

The weeks passed and Guelfo got worse. Frequently he didn't even turn up at school. And when he did go, he played the role of the revolutionary. He repeated Lorenzo's ideas without understanding them and without fully believing them. It seemed as though he wanted to live in his brother's place, or that by copying him he would in some way keep him alive. That was the last year of school, and the final exams were coming up. The literature teacher spoke to Guelfo and told him not to neglect his studies, despite the grief.

But Guelfo couldn't do it. Even the simplest things – like getting dressed, leaving the house, walking, talking to other people – cost him an incredible effort. Francesca approached him again. Since the peace handshake, they had exchanged only a few hellos and numerous looks.

'I haven't got my bike. Could you give me a lift home?' she asked.

'Sure, but I haven't got a helmet for you.'

'Don't worry. After one o'clock you can't find a traffic warden for love nor money.'

'Ok, well I won't wear one either then.' It had come out spontaneously, without thinking. It was almost as if, in some obscure way, he felt that if they shared the same danger they could also share the same fate. They climbed onto the motorbike and Guelfo screeched off as was his habit, so that Francesca had to hold on tight to avoid falling. Guelfo felt her hands tense on his stomach, her arms wrapped around his sides, and the soft and heavy contact of her breast when he braked. Francesca's head bounced on his shoulder and her hair and her fragrance struck him full in the face. He was so profoundly disturbed that he clutched the handlebars desperately, amazed that he hadn't fallen. And after all those days and weeks of hell, life began to flow through him again. A gush, a stream of life, spurting like a wound, which drowned him completely from head to toe and then rose again like heat, pulsing through him. And it all came from those small clenched hands, those locked fingers pressing against him.

'Francesca, I love you, I love you. I've always loved you, and now I know.' This was the thought echoing incessantly in his head as the motorbike charged forward. It flew along between the walls of the narrow streets and darted between the houses; or else it was stopped and the houses were tumbling towards it. Guelfo didn't know. He didn't know anything anymore, and he knew everything. He knew that they could go and smash into that orange bus if he didn't brake. And he had a great desire not to brake, because his life had come to completion in an instant. That girl clinging to him from behind was all that he had to defend. Without her nothing was worth anything, while to die with her was the most beautiful thing in the world. Shall I brake? No! I won't brake and it'll all be over: my parents, Lorenzo, all the shit that await us tomorrow and in the years to come, all the problems that will kill this moment of perfect happiness. 'And what if she doesn't love me?' No she did love him. He was as sure of that as of the air that he breathed, even without having turned round to look at her. It was the only thing he was sure of.

The foot had braked on its own. They had swerved in front of the bus, and in two minutes they were in front of Francesca's door. They had rocked on the now stopped motorbike, panting, incapable of disentangling themselves. They had separated for a second and then embraced again, standing, leaning against one another so as not to fall, with legs that could barely hold them up. They had whispered each other's names and exchanged tiny little kisses, on the face, on the neck on the hands. Then Guelfo could take it no longer, and all the tension of those terrible days, such harsh and unexpected trials, dissolved into tears, into deep sobs drowned in Francesca's hair. She dragged him in through the door, then up the stairs as far as the apartment, still embracing each other.

'No wait, what about your parents. I don't want them to see me like this.'

'There's no-one here, idiot. Daddy's away today. I planned this whole ambush.'

Francesca had lived in that apartment since she was born. It had been left to her father Giovanni by an uncle who had never married. It occupied the entire top floor of an old building, with lots of windows overlooking the square and the same number overlooking the courtyard, towards Borgo Tegolaio. An internal staircase led up to another large room, with windows all round. This was the studio where the uncle had painted, which her parents had transformed into their bedroom. There was a door leading from the room onto a terrace full of flowers, amidst the rooftops.

The front of the apartment was uninterruptedly penetrated by the life of the square, with its noises and smells, the green foliage of the trees, the slightly flaking ochre yellow of the facade of the church, the elegant slender profile of the belltower and the little cupola with its crescent-shaped tiles. The square was intensively inhabited, day and night: it was a world in itself, a port, a market. The apartment was always full of sunlight, lighting the old pastel-coloured walls of pink, blue and yellow that had been masterfully painted by Gino, a Neapolitan friend of Giovanni's, who mixed the pigments himself.

The furniture included lots of period pieces: paintings, family portraits, old sofas, ancient vases, walnut tables, painted sideboards and silver candelabra. It was clear that these items were irreplaceable; they belonged to the world of memories. They came from the past, from the generations that had gone before, and were merely loaned for the use of the current owners, who had the specific duty of conserving them intact for those who would come after. This was why they were not mere objects, but part of a collective soul, in which Giovanni and Francesca lived immersed, accurately recalling faces, names and stories that dated back as far as the end of the eighteenth century. It was, of course, a middle-class home, but of the time when the values of the middle class were still "possess and conserve" rather than this terrible produce and consume.

Giovanni had spent his entire life putting together the lost things of the family. He had sought them out in the houses of grandparents, uncles and aunts and cousins. Sometimes they gave them to him, other times he paid twice what they were worth. But for him, being able to write at the desk that had belonged to your great-grandfather, was something you could not put a price on. Tracing with your hand the little marks made by time on the old wood, thinking that other hands would do the same two hundred years later. And he made other purchases to expand this heritage: he bought beds for Laura and himself and for Francesca, and seventeenth-century corner cupboards at the Pandolfini auction house. He could not bear to live amidst things that were not unique as well as beautiful. He hated serial, industrially-produced objects, with that cold and impersonal design that seemed to freeze a room with their presence alone. They were dumb objects, which it was pointless to listen to. He hated the disposable and he hated waste; not only of things, but of words too, of feelings, of people. In a world without a soul everything became superfluous. You started by throwing away an old chair – because it would cost more to repair it than to buy a new one – and you ended up changing your husband or your wife. Just for the hell of it. To add a frisson to your life. Giovanni, who had always been generous and spent everything he earned, had rediscovered the value of parsimony, of a sober, more precise and elegant way of life. He realised the truth of it every day, with his patients: people who were stressed by commitments, drowning in things, who for an hour would flood him with words most of which they didn't know the meaning of.

'Less, less, less!' he would say, inviting them to reduce the pace of their lives, to give value to what they had. 'If you think about it, the news is generally bad. Happiness lies in routine, for those who know how to grasp it.' He believed that all the beauty of the world was to be found in a vase of flowers, or in an old jug – as Giorgio Morandi had shown – and of course in nature, always. A penetrating fragrance of fresh flowers, gathered in huge bunches, would permeate all the rooms, together with the essence of potpourri from the ancient pharmacy of Santa Maria Novella. The apartment was full of books: in the large bookcase, on top of the furniture, in the bedrooms, even on the floor, in the corridors and in the bathrooms. Books of poetry, essays, hundreds of novels, all the classics and the entire *cursus honorum* of the Marxist culture, and obviously lots of books on psychology: Giovanni's stock-in-trade.

'You haven't read them, have you? Just as well!' Giovanni said to Guelfo a few months later, when he surprised him leafing through some volumes of Marx. 'They're certainly heavy-going, and that's a deterrent, but at times they're also fascinating. There's the danger of falling in love and swallowing the whole thing hook, line and sinker. That's what happened to a lot of my friends, many years ago. I remember one of them, Guido De Masi: he read the whole lot, in German to boot! Instead they ought to be taken like religious books: people know about them because they're common knowledge, and can even quote from them sometimes, but at bottom they don't believe them. Or even if they do believe, they can't follow them. They know that they couldn't do it without ruining their lives, without devoting their entire lives to it. There's something unnatural about these absolute theories, these ideologies, something that runs counter to the essence of human nature. We can't expect to force life to run through these artificial channels. Although having said that, to date man hasn't managed to organise any society that did not revolve around the idea of God.

The worst thing that Marxism – communism – did was to steal the lives of the best young people of the twentieth century. Four generations have paid a high price to this Moloch, to this notion of justice and equality, committing themselves without let or hindrance, sacrificing everything in the illusion of creating a better world. What a terrible waste!But then you also have to think of what happened in the Eastern countries after the fall... Hundreds of thousands of people handed over to a lumpen capitalism, prey to an even greater material and moral misery. The mafia in the place of communism. No, democracy on its own is definitely not enough. Voting can be a very beautiful thing, especially for peoples who have never had elections, but voting alone is pointless unless a society is founded on values.'

Giovanni was about sixty when Guelfo first met him. He hardly ever went out, assisted by the fact that his work as a psychologist could be done at home. It was so reassuring to know that you could always find him there, always affable with everyone. In actual fact, for some time now Giovanni had been following the teaching of Voltaire at the end of *Candide*: 'We must cultivate our own garden'. In the morning he restricted himself to a few rituals. He would go out and have breakfast at the Ricchi bar, then buy the newspaper at the corner and do his shopping in the local shops. His world had contracted to a few dozen metres around his home, and he was delighted with the situation. Especially since all the traffic had become electric. He had everything he needed right there: the Santo Spirito bookshop, which he had set up a few years back with some of his friends, the Sunday markets, the Eolo and Goldoni cinemas, the Goldoni theatre, the trattorias run by his friends Bibo and Beppe. Even Piazza Pitti seemed a long way off to him, distant above all from his vision of the world: it was always so packed with tourists, and with take-away pizza bars and ghastly currency exchanges. For the same reason, during the day he avoided Ponte Vecchio and Ponte Santa Trinita, and only ever crossed them at night, better still in winter when they resumed all their dignified beauty.

He relied on Francesca to perform on his behalf what was required by bureaucracy and the possession of a tax code. There were a lot of things he simply refused to do, and for a long time had simply failed to respond to the numerous categorical invitations that arrived from this or that office. He'd realised that it wasn't a matter of life or death. When things got sticky he could resort to his lawyer friend, who had his studio just a few yards away. 'It's quicker for me to come straight to you, than to reply to them', he'd explain.

Guelfo was enchanted by this world that was so different from his own home, with the shoe repair shops to be managed and the constant breathless rush, the arguments, the slammed doors, the telephone that was always engaged, the time that was never enough and the money that was the constant subject of discussion. Giovanni helped him with this too.

'You see, Guelfo, you have to try to see things from your parents' point of view. They have given you everything they could, in their own way, and consistently with the way they see things. And believe me, when you're accustomed to a high standard of living, when you have to bring home lots of money to meet all those demands that by now seem indispensable, you create a prison around yourself: a prison without bars, but just as terrible nevertheless. The much-reviled shopkeepers are really the heirs of the great merchants. But Florence is not the same as it was in the Renaissance. Now, with a few exceptions, only the dregs of that great entrepreneurial mentality remain. And you should be happy when things are going alright, like in your home. There are lots of people who have to bend over backwards to pay the bills at the end of the month, resorting to post-dated cheques. I can assure you that in these conditions, many people are prepared to make deals with the devil, let alone with the parties or the masons, as has been the practice in this city for so long. Handling money, as you can see, is a major commitment, and it can be very dangerous. You have to keep that constantly in mind, before you pass judgement, especially when you're accustomed to getting your wages from the State. And besides, the biggest scourge at present is unemployment, and since the world was made the only people to create jobs have been the businessmen.'

Guelfo spent more and more time with Francesca. As soon as school was over, he'd grab something to eat at home and rush over to her house. They were studying for their last-year exams together, since when his schoolwork had immediately improved.

He had long chats with Giovanni, who had taken to him immediately, happy to see Francesca so radiant. It was, in a way, a sort of therapy, although not openly declared as such. Guelfo was in need of help, and Giovanni had got into the habit of letting him come into his studywhen he had finished with his few patients. There, as he put his things in order, he would let Guelfo talk and he would listen. The study was a big room at the back of the apartment, with a desk pushed up against the wall. It was crammed full of so many books, objects and bric-a-brac that you could hardly see the walls. There was an old violin and two fencing foils, complete with competition masks, a ripped ship's pennant and an army of lead soldiers. Giovanni had even hung on the wall the old bicycle that he no longer used. There was a telescope in one corner and a Napoleonic camp bed in another. In contrast to the care and extreme good taste lavished on the rest of the apartment, the study was deliberately neglected. It was almost as if its occupant were so wrapped up in his alchemical distillations that he didn't have time for anything else. It looked as though the remains of a shipwreck had been randomly swept together there by storm winds.

Guelfo entered the room with a certain trepidation and great curiosity. God knows why, but it reminded him of the belly of the whale and he saw himself as Jonah, with a candle in his hand setting off to explore it. He felt as if he had returned to the mythical age, when the magma of the passions was at full boil and men were learning how to be men. Discovering love, hate, revenge, generosity, all still fused and meshed together. Years later, thinking back to these images, he realised how accurate they'd been. In that room Guelfo had learnt to look at the world with different eyes, to look into himself. He had begun his journey through the myriad consequences of knowledge in a search that was to continue for ever. He would sit down on the revolving leather chair, and Giovanni would prompt him, saying, 'What do you want to talk about today?', turning his back to Guelfo and fiddling around with his clocks, his patients' records, photographs and a huge number of pieces of paper bearing indecipherable scribbles. Every so often he would get up to go to the telephone which he kept in the room next door. In his absence, Guelfo would observe the incredible clutter of the room more closely, trying to find some logical order, but he couldn't. The truth was that the study was a representation of Giovanni's unconscious, the secret and dark part of his life. Every time he left it, he would lock the door. He wouldn't allow anyone to clean it. When he was engaged in something particularly interesting, he would remain there for even two or three days at a time, sleeping fully dressed on the camp bed for a few hours and surviving on sandwiches. To leave his cave would have distracted him, and he would have lost his concentration. Francesca would see him emerge eventually, red-eyed with a few days' stubble on his chin.

'So it's the Nobel this time then?'

But Giovanni was unpredictable: he might start from the reworking of some old recipe, say *cailles en sarcophage* and end up classifying various grasses that he found in the fields at the side of the old road to Pozzolatico. Or he would have programmed, down to the tiniest detail, a sailing trip to the Azores to be taken the following summer in his little boat. He would chart the ports, moorings, anchorages, miles, knots, winds, leeway, isobars, and bone up on the restaurants, the anecdotes, traditions, language, dialects and curiosities of the places he would stop at. A journey that, naturally, he would never actually make.

V

Laura had arrived in Florence in the middle of the 1990s. She was Brazilian and came from Rio da Janeiro, where she had left behind her a marriage that hadn't worked out. She was thirty years old, and although she was qualified as an architect she had never practised, having been spoiled first by her wealthy parents and then by her surgeon husband. She'd decided to come to Florence for a change of air, to take some time out to think – and a year's painting course was exactly what she needed.

She was tall, with long legs and long arms and large hands. She was supple, and had a sort of slow, dark beauty that people found intimidating but which she carried confidently. The sudden end of her marriage had taken her by surprise. The affair that her husband had had with an insignificant secretary seemed as ridiculous as it was impossible. She had left within the space of a few hours, too offended and too proud to go into the matter further. As she returned to her parents' house, she thought back with amazement at that last scene with her husband. Humiliated, he had begged her to stay, and then as she left he had shouted after her. 'Ok. So I made a mistake. But have you ever asked yourself what you've given me in these five years? Nothing! Leftovers! You're an idol, you're incapable of love. You're an emotional cripple!'

Laura hadn't understood. Having at your side a beautiful, elegant, perfumed woman, who was the envy of all, what on earth more could you possibly want? Laura knew everyone who was anyone. She was a superb hostess, helping her husband in his career. It was true she hadn't wanted children, not yet anyway. And just as well, she reflected now. Did she love Carlos? It was a question that, to be quite honest, she didn't really know the answer to. Certainly she hadn't loved him as she'd loved Luciano, but her behaviour had always been irreprehensible, despite all the admirers who continually flocked around her.

Luciano had died at the age of twenty in an underwater spearfishing accident. Try as she might, Laura could not get that terrible afternoon at Angra dos Reis out of her head. He had dived in, leaving her on the boat sunbathing. A minute later he'd surfaced again, holding out to her an immense starfish. He had dived again, and a short time later had floated to the surface, unconscious. They were completely alone in a remote bay. Laura had dragged him back onto the boat and had begun a frenetic mouth-to-mouth resuscitation, alternated with a furious cardiac massage. She was too far from any hospital or first aid clinic. If she wanted to save him, she would have to do it on her own. She'd gone on trying for more than an hour: an interminably long, desperate hour. Her eyes were bloodshot for weeks afterwards: in the effort to breathe life back into Luciano's body she broken all the capillaries. All she could remember were the raucous calls of dozens of parrots perched in the trees that hung over the water around the bay. In the end she'd fainted, exhausted and defeated.

That day, a part of her had died along with Luciano. Carlos had not succeeded in healing her; she hadn't allowed him to. Having suffered so much pain, she had unconsciously decided to live on the surface of things. She had studied well and she had married well, doing everything in the best possible way, always according to the rules. But she had never again plunged her hands into life. In that sense Carlos was right.

She thought about it again when she arrived in Florence, looking at the Arno from the terrace of the apartment that she had rented in Borgo San Jacopo. She'd always been attracted by Florence. According to her, Rio de Janeiro was the most beautiful city in the world in natural terms. Nowhere else could you find such dazzlingly white beaches, such striking coves and then the huge bay, sixty kilometres deep, which the Portuguese had mistaken for a river, calling it Rio de Janeiro, the river of January, after the month when they had found it. And then there were the unexpected mountains of black lava stone, rising to a height of eight hundred metres just a few yards from the sea: the Corcovado, the Sugarloaf Mountain, the Dois Irmãos, Pedra da Gávea. The unique vegetation: an Atlantic forest extending in and around the city, creating deep shade for the streets with its large heavy leaves. A tropical forest where lots of animals still lived, and large trees with their Guaraní names: *ipê, jacarandá, peroba, jequitibá, umbaúba and juquiri.*

Florence was, instead, without a doubt the most beautiful built city. It was a hymn to the intelligence, harmony and rationality of the great Renaissance. It was an unbelievable concentrate of art, and yet it didn't crush you. You could live in the midst of it; you were an agent of it, it was made to your measure. This was the most wonderful aspect, the great secret. Intelligently, the Medici had protected it in the seventeenth century, even from the splendid Baroque, so as not to alter its perfect equilibrium. In Florence you could easily live in palazzi which, elsewhere in the world, would have been museums. You could buy ice-cream or go to eat in trattorias that were in the very places where Ghiberti or Ghirlandaio had had their workshops.

Leon Battista Alberti's theory had been that, ideally, every city should be home to everyone, and every house a little city. For a long time this had been possible in Florence, and it still was to a degree in the Oltrarno, where Laura had chosen to live. Giovanni had spotted her one spring morning from his window, crossing the square and setting up her easel almost in the centre, opposite the church. Laura was wearing a simple tunic of light blue wool which reached as far as her ankles. On her feet she wore beige tennis shoes and on her head a straw hat to protect her from the sun. Giovanni had gone on watching her, captivated. Laura's figure filled the space, as if the square had suddenly somehow become smaller. Then he went down the stairs in a strange state of nervous agitation. He passed close to her as he went to the newsagent's, and then retraced his steps settling himself behind her perched on the rim of the fountain, leafing through the newspaper without seeing even the headlines. Laura's beauty enveloped him like a magnetic field. He stared at the shape of her broad shoulders beneath the light fabric, and her strong slender neck with the long black hair gathered at the nape, under the hat. Her hands, which moved with the brush, cut the air.

Giovanni had reached the age of forty-five without having sorted out his love life. After a few youthful passions, which had left no trace other than tender memories, he had fallen in love with a married woman with two children. They had been together twelve years. It was a neurotic relationship with constant ups and downs, and it had taken Giovanni many years to realise that she and her husband would never leave each other. Even though they each lived their own lives, in their way they were still a couple, a family. And in the end it was always he who was left on his own – at Christmas, at Easter, during the summer holidays. Giovanni had so many interests that he used these periods of freedom to read, to study and to travel. Especially on foot: if there was a part of his body that he loved it was his legs, which were strong and never got tired. But, in the end, he'd realised how crazy and sterile this relationship was, and he'd succeeded in calling a halt, finding himself at the age of forty with nothing to show, drained. After that nothing of any significance had happened, and he'd grown to accept it. There were so many interesting things in life that one could be happy just the same. And, at the end of the day, he wasn't really cut out for the classic middle-class marriage, or for children.

But now, he simply had to get to know this girl, and he didn't know how to set about it. He'd heard her speaking, trying to free herself of another admirer who was trying to chat her up with the excuse of discussing painting. She had a strong voice, with deep tones, and expressed herself in an Italian that was already quite confident. He had realised with relief, from her accent, that she wasn't American. Giovanni was profoundly Latin, and he found himself at his ease in those countries and with those peoples. Perhaps it was on account of the common Catholic matrix that bound them, for better or for worse. While the evident superiority of the Protestants in constructing a State and governing it with simpler and more efficient rules was undeniable.

Giovanni was shy and he didn't know where to begin. He went to have a coffee and he put his predicament to Enzo.

'How do you go about it? Easily I'd say! Are you really that interested in her? Well she certainly is a looker... Leave it to me.' It was nearly twelve o'clock, and Enzo had a magnificent table set out, right beside the fountain. With white tablecloths, a huge bunch of calla lilies rapidly procured from the florist's stall, and on the table wine, bread, broad beans, pecorino cheese, raw ham and fruit. Then he called his wife, Andrea the greengrocer, Giada the tobacconist, a couple of customers who were drinking at the bar, two antiquarians and a gilder. As soon as the bells began to ring out twelve o'clock, Enzo announced:

'Today is the twenty-fourth of April and it is the feast of Pentecost and therefore the feast of the Piazza of Santo Spirito, and we are celebrating it as we do every year. Salute! Good health! Young lady, would you like to drink something with us?' and so saying he handed Laura a glass of wine. Then he said in an undertone to Giovanni: 'Don't be a fool, and you can pass by later to pay me.' Laura could not refuse; on the contrary she accepted willingly. For the rest of her life she remembered that moment with great joy. She had become a Florentine.

Giovanni wasn't handsome. It was something he'd never paid any attention to. But he had charm. And he was a brilliant and captivating conversationalist. He could talk for hours about anything, serious or lightweight, and people would listen to that wonderful voice of his without ever getting tired. It was a gift he knew he had. Often, for the most varied problems, he would say to his friends 'Let me speak to him.' And rarely were matters not resolved.

Giovanni talked to Laura for two whole months, without letting her go for a second, lost as he was in that gaze of hers that had stolen his destiny. He took her out, showed her Florence and they went on long walks in the surrounding area. They went to dinner everywhere, and the enthusiasm was contagious. But he never summoned up the courage to make a proposal. Towards the end of June, it was Laura who asked him, 'Will you take me to Sardinia? I've never been, and everyone tells me it's beautiful.'

'Wonderful!' replied Giovanni. 'What do you say to going on a boat?'

The *Gone with the Wind* was moored at Porto Santo Stefano. It was an old boat of little more than nine metres, laden with glory and extremely uncomfortable. They spent ten days on it. Two hundred and forty long hours of sun, sea, salt, spaghetti in all possible sauces, long swims. Sailing in the Bocche di Bonfacio, with the gunwale in the water, feet in the cockpit and the bar held fast with four hands and arms tensed. 'Watch out, we're turning, draw in, draw in!' In the evening they would anchor in the little coves, away from everyone, perfectly alone. That's where Francesca was born. It was just that she only emerged nine months later, exactly when the Hale-Bopp comet passed. And Laura had been born again: she had tied up the scattered threads of her life, finally casting off that stone that had been weighing on her heart for over ten years.

As they returned to Florence, it was she who had asked. 'Where shall we go, your place or mine?' considering that, after those ten days, they couldn't possibly leave each other.

'Wherever you want, but from tomorrow I'm moving in with you, and you – architect – have to begin organising our home. Now it has to house a family.'

After fifteen years, Laura had left. It was long-thought-out, conscious, difficult decision. And she was aware that by taking it she was putting everything on the line. What she couldn't understand was that she was the prisoner of a perverse mechanism, which nothing could hold out against. She'd talked about it endlessly with Giovanni. Long, exhausting discussions, almost always late at night, when Francesca was sleeping.

One day he'd brought home the video of an old film, a science-fiction classic called *Forbidden Planet*. It was the story of a space mission launched to discover the fate of another expedition sent ten years earlier and lost without trace. When the spaceship landed on the planet, the crew found the only survivors: the scientist who had been in charge of the earlier expedition and his young daughter. They were told how an invisible monster had killed all the other astronauts, although since then for some years everything had been calm. But with the arrival of the new spaceship, the killings recommence. The monster, which is pure force, kills them one by one. In the end only the professor, his daughter and the captain of the spaceship are left, and have locked themselves into a bunker. The professor activates the safety doors, saying: 'Now we have nothing more to worry about, these special metal panels can resist all attacks, all temperatures.'

Then the blond captain, in his shiny 50s-style spacesuit, shouts at him: 'So you still haven't understood? That it's your mind, your unconscious that fuels the energy of the monster? You're afraid of losing your daughter to another man, and you have created this monster through your own thought, without realising it. Nothing can withstand it: no steel, no weapons. You are responsible for all these deaths.' The professor finally understands, and in despair he kills himself, and at the same time also kills the monster. As a result his daughter and the captain can live happily ever after.

At the end of the film Laura turned to Giovanni and said, 'Good film, but I don't understand how it applies to me? I certainly don't want to kill you to stop you being with Francesca!'

'No, Laura! That's not the way it should be read, and I'm not surprised that you don't understand. You're up to your neck in this thing, and the sick part of you tends to self-defence. Here it's not a question of whether you love me or not, even though obviously that's a crucial aspect. The point is that no-one can make you happy – not me, not Francesca, nor anyone else – unless you're willing to help yourself. You could live in the most beautiful house in the world, have more money that you knew how to spend. Maybe you'd dream of escaping with a penniless Greek sailor and going to live on nothing on a desert island. This negative ego of yours puts a pressure on anyone sharing your life that is impossible to bear. This is the monster of the film that overcomes all obstacles. There is no real life, however splendid, that can be enough for you. Everything is minced up and swallowed.'

'So what should I do? Kill myself to kill the monster? I've thought about it, you know, but it doesn't seem like such a great idea.'

'Well, that's certainly what he wants. He would prefer to die with you, rather than to be driven out and perish alone. I'm speaking metaphorically, but only up to a point.'

Nothing made any difference. Laura had made up her mind, with death in her heart together with the pride and despair of being loved by such a wonderful man as Giovanni, and not loving him in return. Or rather of no longer loving him: she still felt affection, as well as empathy and esteem, but the love had disappeared, suddenly, almost without warning.

In recent years Laura had begun to feel useless. Francesca was at school until five in the afternoon. Giovanni was content, immersed in his gratifying work and caught up for days at a time in his multiple interests. Everyone was living full lives, except her, and she had practically nothing at all to do. She'd never got used to housekeeping, and she did it reluctantly. She'd even tried working, but her degree wasn't recognised in Italy, and she'd had to make do with designing a few gardens. She went home every August and every Christmas. Giovanni couldn't always go with her, and indeed every so often made up an excuse so that he wouldn't have to. It wasn't that he didn't like Rio – it was impossible not to – but he felt strangely threatened by it. Something told him that one day Laura might return there for ever.

'It's your home,' he would reassure her. 'There are your parents, who see so little of you now, your friends. Don't worry about me. I'm happy for you to go.'

Three years earlier Laura's father had fallen seriously ill, and Laura had had to leave suddenly, and on her own; Francesca had school. She'd stayed for three months, going back to her old life: being waited on hand and foot by the numerous servants. With breakfast served at the side of the pool in the morning, the sea view and the beija-flores hovering in the air to suck the nectar from the multicoloured flowers. Her father was on the mend, and so was Laura. She even found herself singing as she got ready to go out. She was like a girl again. She went out with her friends and bought herself the most stunning clothes. Her mother had unlimited credit everywhere. She spent hours on end having treatments in beauty salons, chatting and laughing like crazy at all the gossip that she had to catch up with: who's married who, who's left who, who's bedding who... And everywhere she went she felt something like a veiled reproof, even from her manicurist.

'Laurinha, what are you doing in Italy? You of all people, with all the money your parents have. Look at your hands! They look like a maid's. Nobody can make any sense of it.'

The truth of the matter was that they didn't really take much to Giovanni. Deprived of his prime asset, conversation, which in another language lost most of its charm, he didn't have a lot going for him in the eyes of the cariocas. He wasn't rich; he wasn't noble (for the Brazilians, all Italians of a certain type ought to be counts at least); he wasn't even very tall. And he had carried off Laurinha, which had been a great loss for Rio. Added to this was the fact that Giovanni could not completely conceal a certain intellectual contempt for these wealthy people, who were frequently ignorant and false, besotted with luxury and excess. Instead of going out with Laura's friends, Giovanni preferred to go round Rio on his own. It was the only metropolis he knew where in many places a village atmosphere continued to exist. Strange as it might seem, it was still possible to live there in complete tranquillity. For example, on the beach, which was populated by all kinds of people, or in the thousands of little bars in the streets off Leblon and Ipanema, where you could drink the best beer in the world, always ice-cold. Then there was the smell of grilled meat, fried onion and salt cod balls at every hour of the day and night, and the incredibly dense, colourful fruit juices: *manga, maracu-*

já, conde, cajù, goiaba. Amazing music blared out from thousands of radios, which appeared to be hidden somewhere in the air. Giovanni would spend weeks wearing clogs and bathing shorts, with a towel flung over his shoulders and a little money stashed in a tiny pocket. He was totally absorbed by watching this humanity so different from what he knew: the incredible mixture of races, and the direst poverty living cheek-by-jowl with the brashest wealth, somehow without clashing.

He was entranced by the grace of the Brazilian people, by the cheerful way they performed even the hardest jobs, by the light touch with which they dealt with the evil of life. Despite the violence, the inequality and the low expectations of the future, despite the centuries-long exploitation by the Portuguese, like that of the Spaniards in the rest of Latin America. It was, as the great landscape architect Burle Marx justly said, a people who knew neither Leonardo nor Dante, neither Bach nor Chopin. The Brazilians were a people who had suffered, full of pain, but had nevertheless managed to develop their own notion of beauty. There was a harmony expressed in the Carnival, in the costumes, in the way the girls spoke and moved, in the samba. The film *Black Orpheus* was an emblematic example of it. It was a natural beauty that Giovanni discovered when talking to people, watching them sing the latest pop song accompanying themselves with two empty cans, observing the matches of football and foot-volley on the beach. He saw it in the gesture of the young black opening an iced coconut by striking it rapidly with a large knife, then offering it on the open palm of his hand: '*Pronto, senhor!*'

He enjoyed himself so much that sometimes darkness had already fallen by the time he got home, still wearing his bathing shorts. He adored that hot tropical air, striking him in the face. Laura wouldn't even wait for him. She'd leave instructions for him to join her at someone or other's house. Francesca, already in her pyjamas, would remind him, telling him off: 'Mummy was really cross!'

'Never mind, darling,' Giovanni would reply. 'To-morrow we'll go to the beach and to the Jardim Botanico. We're going to have such fun. Listen to what I learned today, sing along with me *Vai meu irmão, pega esse avião, você tem razão de correr assim deste frio...*', beating time with his hands on his mother'-in-law's colonial table and, as he was well aware, earning her contempt. In fact, the next morning she complained to her daughter, *'Laura este seu marido não presta.'*

This was the time of his friendship with Sandro, a Roman who had been in voluntary exile in Rio for twenty-five years, whose sole concern in life appeared to be the attempt to achieve perfection in various salads made by combining local and Mediterranean vegetables. In addition to the Scotch nectar of Messrs. Justerini and Brooks, which he imbibed in industrial quantities. Giovanni had won him over by bringing him new olive oil from the mill every year at Christmas and by taking a great interest in the basil, tomatoes, rocket, mixed salad and chicory that Sandro grew in huge tubs on his balcony, which were closely guarded by a toucan with an incredible yellow beak.

'How do you think they're coming on this year?' Sandro would ask him with the abstracted air of a planter, as if he had thousands of hectares of coffee or cocoa.

'Definitely very well. It all seems delicious to me.'

'You're just saying that to please me. But don't you feel that the flavour isn't quite right? That this basil with these huge leaves, isn't even related to ours? Despite all my efforts! In some of the tubs I've even got soil from the Pontine marshes that I got an Alitalia captain to bring me in sacks. It's a wonder he wasn't arrested for drug smuggling. And then the tomatoes! Splendid from outside, but pale inside.'

'They seem fine to me,' Giovanni reassured him.

'That's the oil, the oil. With this oil of yours even a shoe would taste good. The proverb really says it all: *Brazil, the land of odourless flowers, tasteless fruit and shameless women.*'

'It seems to me that you're taken considerable advantage of that last quality. Judging from the comings and goings in this house...'

Pedagogy, pure pedagogy, Giovanni. I'm screwing the daughters and nieces of the women I frequented when I first came here. Since I'm a gentleman, and I always treated them all accordingly, every so often they bring me a wench: "Doctor, we have this girl at home, why don't you keep her for a bit and teach her something. How to eat, how to dress, how to talk. She's a good girl, she'll keep everything in order for you".'

'Yes, yes! I have a pretty good idea what they keep in order for you...'

'Giovanni, I'm surprised at you! For many of these poor wretches the only alternative would have been walking the streets. Believe me, they're much better off here. Last year I pulled off my masterpiece. Do you remember that Roman prince who spent a few weeks here as my guest, that I introduced you to? Well he took a great fancy to that girl Paula who was here in the house at the time, that cute half-caste. A month after he left, he phoned me and asked if I could send her to him in Rome for a while. Naturally he would take care of everything. And so it went. Well, now he's married her. Fantastic, don't you think? Straight from the Vidigal favela to the Black Aristocracy of Rome, complete with palazzo, doorman and chauffeur. Paula will become the queen, the patron saint of the thousands of Brazilian women who have followed Italian plumbers, pensioners, bakers and sales reps, the prick emigration! As a talent scout I'm better than Pygmalion.'

'There's no denying it,' admitted Giovanni.

'I can see you don't approve.'

'It's not that. It's just that I have a different idea about relationships with women, or rather, with one woman.'

'Giovanni, I don't think you know very much about women at all. Take it from someone who does know a thing or two about them. I was like you once: the beautiful house, the beautiful wife, the office. A mosaic with all the pieces in their right places. Then, when my father died so young, I suffered a trauma. I asked myself what this whole pantomime meant, what was in it for me. And so I ran away, to Africa, to Senegal. After three years the Church tracked me down. Two missionaries suddenly appeared out of nowhere in a jeep and they handed over to me the sentence of annulment from the Sacra Rota, obtained by a cardinal who was my wife's uncle. Since then, I've lived as I do now, and I like it. In any case, it's not worth the trouble, nothing's worth the trouble. And so I live for the moment. The essence of life can be encapsulated in a really good salad or between the legs of a stranger, in her sweat, in her hoarse gasping. Everything is in the moment. A pure diamond with seven lights, always different. Just like women.'

'A prism drowned in whisky, Sandro. An illusion.'

'Everything's an illusion, Giovanni. I know that you think I'm throwing away my life with this low-class Bohème of mine, and that it's pathetic for a man of fifty-seven. But I can assure you that in my life the tragedy far outweighs the comedy, although to be honest they're often mingled. I have gout and cirrhosis and I find it hard to lace up my shoes. I live on the generosity of my mother; she's got inventing pretexts to send me money without humiliating me down to a fine art. There are a few Italian friends who give me a hand, entrusting to me the decor of parts of their homes. Small stuff, though. And of course they're right, because frequently I take the advances and don't deliver the work. Just think, a couple of years ago they organised an exhibition of all the cheques they'd cashed for me and that I then failed to pay. They were all framed: minor masterpieces, and some of them extremely rare, such as a Banco Nacional from just after I arrived, lots of ITAÚ, and a few from the Banco Frances-Italiano, which no longer exists. Sandro even went through a pink period, with the Bradesco bank, with its hallmark pink cheques. And I've certainly done some wild things in my time. Like that dinner on Christmas Day that you were at too, as well as Laura, Silvano and Claudio, do you remember? I got you all roaring drunk and we were still there at two o'clock in the morning, and I made a pass at the cook. Or that time at the official lunch, when I threw the ambassador and another seven or eight guests into the swimming pool.'

'I like the story of that truck driver from Piedmont who invited you to dinner and served you *Veuve Cliquot* all evening, extolling its virtues and what good value it was. And you told him that, since he was obviously a connoisseur, you might well be able to procure for him a few rare bottles of *Monsieur Cliquot*, from the time when the widow's husband was still alive, and he immediately gave you a thousand dollars.'

'Yes!! What a laugh! What an idiot! But the truth is that they put up with me because they like having me around. I am one of the few well-bred Italians of the Rio colony. People come from god knows where to seek their fortunes, most of whom have forgotten Italian without having learned Portuguese. Every time they have an important dinner, they ask for my help. They go wild about my Roman friends who every so often come to visit me, especially when they're aristocrats or cinema people.

'Well, no-one could say you haven't enjoyed yourself...'

'That's for sure. And I already have my epitaph ready:

Just imagine that on the tombstone! And believe me, that's how it should be: play the funny man right to the end, you have to be consistent. Don't delude yourself, you either. Not even about your magnificent Laura, who hates me. She, so perfect...'

'She told me that you tried to kiss her in the kitchen the second time we came to dinner here.'

'It was just a gesture of affection towards you, Giovanni, after the usual six-scotch cocktail. A sudden inspiration. And you have to admit that her neck is certainly more attractive than yours. Nothing erotic about it at all. Just as well you understood that, otherwise you wouldn't be here.'

'Of course I understood, that and a lot more besides. I don't judge you. On the contrary, if I did have to express an opinion it would probably be flattering, seeing that I spend more time here with you that at my in-laws' house. But it saddens me. Always this whisky: it's an obsession.'

'As Vinicius de Moraes, our poet who after his death became a street, used to say:

> if a dog is a man's best friend,
> whisky is a dog in a bottle.

Come on, let's make this salad and then we'll go and stretch our legs. What books have you brought me this year?'

'The Florentines Luzi and Bigongiari, the latest, seeing as you read only poetry. Good stuff! I don't know if they're the ones Pratolini invoked when he hoped that finally the wombs of our women would give birth to the fully-fledged poet that Florence had been awaiting for centuries. I think he had another Dante in mind. And Dante is not repeatable. But these are certainly very worthwhile...'

'I trust your judgement. Especially after you brought me Eliot's *Four Quartets*, which I didn't know. Wonderful! By the way, you know that painter friend of yours who came to visit me last summer? Quite a drinker, by Jove! He writes poems, and they're not at all bad. He just tossed one off at my house one evening. It begins like this: "I walk barefoot/on long black beaches covered in flowers/ and fish are born between my hands...".'

Day after day, Laura had ended up accepting the advances of a partner of her brother's, a financier, recently divorced. And this affair had gone ahead every time she came back, on her part more as a pastime than out of passion. Recently he had come to visit her almost every month, in Rome at the Hotel d'Angleterre, where he spent a few days, and she found some excuse to come and join him. Now finally, she'd decided. What she had failed to take into consideration was that Francesca wasn't certain she wanted to come with her. Laura had always taken it for granted: children go with the mother, perhaps because she'd already started thinking about this return some years before, when Francesca was still very young and wouldn't have had any choice in the matter.

This time too, it was Giovanni who came to her aid. He convinced her that, in any case, nothing was final, that it was always wise to leave a door open. He resorted to all those illusions people use when they're separating: 'It'll be a trial period; perhaps it'll help us to see things more clearly. Then, after calm consideration, we can decide.' Laura pretended to agree with him, and at that moment she really believed it, as he did himself. Otherwise the pain of cancelling all those years in one fell swoop would have been too much, would have been unbearable. They'd spent the last few months practically without ever going out. At night in bed they clung to each other, silent, with Laura tormented by remorse. But Giovanni had realised that she couldn't stay, not at that time, in that condition: it would have been like having a zombie in the house. His only hope of having Laura back – the real Laura, beautiful, vivacious, stimulating – was to agree to let her go, to give her the courage to leave, now that she didn't have it. He remembered one of the first things he'd studied in psychology: 'you have to succeed in agreeing to your death in order to be born again from your ashes.' And so he'd booked her flight, bought the ticket, packed her bags and accompanied her to the airport.

Francesca had spent the last few days almost entirely in her own room, after she came back from school. Even while they were driving to Fiumicino she sat in the back reading a book with her *walkman* headset on, which a as a rule she never used. She would happily have done without all this.

Despite huge numbers of tranquillisers, as the day of the departure approached Laura had begun to go to pieces. She couldn't do anything; she dropped things and the tears would well up without her realising it. On the morning of her departure she wanted to take their dog Rodrigo for a walk – just the two of them. Giovanni was against it; he was worried about the state she was in, but she insisted. Summoning up all her remaining energy, she got as far as the Forte Belvedere, along the usual route they had followed so many times before. She sat down on a bench with Florence laid out before her. It was a June morning, and the city was so beautiful, with its solid and proud mansions driven into the ground, that in her state of heightened sensibility Laura could hardly breathe. Hugging her dog, her head buried in his curly fur, she thought back to when she had arrived in Florence so many years before. She went back over her meeting with Giovanni, their love, the birth of Francesca: the way she had finally become an adult, a real woman, a person. She saw it all again in a sort of vertigo. 'Oh God, oh Father take this cup away from me. How beautiful it would be to die now, let me die here and now. I can't go on.'

Rodrigo licked her cheeks, and Laura let herself fall onto the grass scattered with daisies, her eyes closed. Of course it would have been easier to throw herself off the rampart. A moment and it would all be over. She saw the treetops and was morbidly attracted by them. No! that would be the last straw. What a wonderful gift for Francesca and Giovanni! They didn't deserve that. And all on account of her neurosis, the death drives inherited from a hysterical mother, all on account of her basic dissatisfaction, her selfishness. These were serious problems that had accompanied her all her life. She'd thought she'd got over them, but she realised that in all these years she'd only exorcised them. 'Is it possible,' Laura asked herself, 'that I haven't managed to build anything at all? That I've eaten, slept, made love, had a child, laughed, cried and dreamed with a man for fifteen years without being able to build anything? That all those bricks I placed day after day have crumbled and sunk into the mud? I have no foundations, I'm not grounded, I'm a miserable wretch.'

Somehow or other she'd managed to make it home. It was late. Giovanni was waiting for her at the corner. He ran towards her, concerned. Her bags were already stowed in the car. Laura had nipped into the house quickly to leave the dog and go to the bathroom. She'd cast her eyes one last time around the home that she'd gathered together with so much love, day after day. In that last glance she sought somehow to take it with her. Once again the memory of all the years passed before her, furrowing her soul with its sharp blade. She'd gone downstairs slowly, holding onto the banister, making a huge effort with every step, since her legs were giving way beneath her. In the hall she leant against the wall, she suddenly felt as if she were going to be sick, but nothing would come. She breathed deeply, once or twice, put on her dark glasses and managed to make the few steps to the car. She didn't speak at all until it was time to say goodbye to Giovanni.

'Giovanni, please come with me, I beg you...', her voice broke on the last word.

He shook his head, smiling sadly, 'Go, go now. You have Francesca with you. If you want you can come back again in two days. I'll be here waiting for you. But now you have to go.'

Laura knew that she wouldn't come back, she knew this was the end. That's why she was so overwrought. But how hard it was, how much it hurt! She was already beyond the gate, and she turned again: 'My love, what will remain of us?'

'Comradeship, for ever'.

It had been too much for Giovanni too. He'd helped her disappear. He'd completed his duty. Now he could think about his own grief. He drove back to Florence, taking it easy. Orvieto, Arezzo, Incisa. The motorway signs loomed up in front of him, illuminated by the headlights, waking him from his reveries. He went back to the apartment, not knowing what to do. For the first time he felt it empty, alien, inimical. He was exhausted but wide awake. This was where he was going to have to live from now on, without Laura, without Francesca. After fifteen years, he removed the two pillows from her side of the bed. Feather pillows: too soft for him. The large wrought-iron bed, painted with angels and clouds, looked amputated without them. It gave him the impression of a catafalque: even the sheets were cold and hostile, hard to open as if they were glued together. Giovanni stretched his legs, lost in that bed that was suddenly too big, where all he could find was his loneliness. He invited Rodrigo to jump up, who was delighted by this unhoped-for treat. He tried to read, but he couldn't. After a couple of hours he took a knock-out sleeping pill.

Suddenly the phone rang.

'Hello Daddy it's me, Francesca. We've just got here. We had a good flight. We're at grandma's house now. Wait, I'll put mummy on.'

Laura's few words, sweet and affectionate, said it all. The instant recognition of tone and minimal nuance that turns all lovers into perfect lie detectors was sufficient to make him realise that for her the worst was over. She was back home, and she had already begun the slow but sure recovery that would distance her from him beyond repair. So now it was she who consoled him, tried to encourage him. In just a few hours the roles had been reversed. Yes. She'd gone home: she had another home. But for him, his home – their home – was where they had lived together. He didn't have another one.

Francesca had returned before planned, after little more than a month. When she arrived at the airport she found her father dramatically changed. He looked as though he had been seriously ill. It was as if Laura had taken away his smile, the little youth that still remained to him, his enthusiasm for life. Francesca had left a father who scarcely looked fifty and returned after a month to find a sixty-year-old, vainly seeking to conceal his sadness. The look in his eyes was different, the tone of his voice, even his way of walking. All this made her love him even more. Her last doubts about where to live, whether to go with mummy – all the self-interested calculations that youngsters make when their parents separate – had dissolved as she looked at him. Somehow she repressed the spontaneous leap of joy, and the cry of 'Daddy! Daddy!' died on her lips. She was suddenly ashamed of her amazing suntan, of her arms full of presents, her new clothes, her hat, her coloured bracelets. In the few metres that still separated them, while the customs officer made a chalk mark on her case, releasing it, Francesca forgot the parties, the beach, that intriguing city and all the beguiling opportunities that had been dangled before her eyes. For the first time, she had taken the body of this man into her young girl's arms; he had let himself go, and she had hugged him in a long and gentle embrace. Then she whispered in his ear, 'I've come back. I'm here now, you don't have to worry. Now there are two of us and we'll be fine.'

This marked the start of a new relationship of total equality. Although she was only fourteen, in a very short time Francesca had taken control of the house and Giovanni was more than happy to let her. He had never been capable of even unblocking a washbasin, and for him changing a light bulb had something of the miraculous. Every so often Francesca would rebuke him for being untidy, for letting his patients smoke in the little sitting-room. Then she'd burst out laughing at herself for sounding so much like a housewife. She had organised the house perfectly, managing with consummate experience to hold her own with the various Italian or Filipino hourly cleaning-ladies. After a year she had found Rina, who lived a stone's throw away in Via Maffia. Rina, who had just retired, was a mine of wisdom, experience and stories. She knew everything about everyone, and everyone loved her. She had an ancient, constant energy, and she was on her feet and on the move from seven in the morning until eleven at night, at which time she punctually went to bed. An hour spent doing nothing was for her not only impossible but a waste of life. Watching the television in the evening, she would always be sewing or knitting. It was amazing the number of things that she could do over the course of the day without ever getting tired.

'There's nothing to it! Leave it, leave it, I'll do that. I'll have it done in a jiffy.' She was a widow with three grown-up children who lived on their own; she rented out two rooms to foreign students, and now she also went to "do" for Francesca. At first she had been bewildered by this child-mistress, but then, little by little, they won each other over. Gradually Francesca handed over all the duties and responsibilities to her, and began to live like a fifteen-year-old girl again.

Guelfo had also discussed the mystery of God with Francesca. She had been attending scouts since the age of eleven, but in a rather half-hearted way: more out of the desire to stay with a group of friends from middle school than out of any deep conviction. She liked the coloured uniforms and the badges and the long walks in the hills that her father had taught her to love. It was only when her parents' marriage was on the rocks that she developed a religious sentiment. She was still strong and whole, but in the evening she would pray desperately that her mother would not leave. After Laura's departure she went on praying that her mother would come back. She had lived through the separation with a strong sense of guilt. Perhaps her mother had left because she was not good enough or because she didn't love her enough. Giovanni let her be. He'd always been brilliantly atheist, and didn't really care much about it one way or the other. He found this replacement of Mummy with the Madonna touching. Francesca had suffered enough: it was only right that she should use any means she wanted to boost her self-preservation. Such as the strange little sacrifices she made. Out of the blue she'd stopped eating chocolate, which she loved. And she'd also become a blood donor. Now that she was older, Francesca in fact looked more kindly on all the activities of the scouts that were connected with charity and voluntary work and solidarity. She had a particular gift for being with the sick, and with people who were different. She regularly attended the Arcobaleno centre in Via del Leone, which had been founded many years earlier by Eugenio Banzi, an extraordinary man and a friend of Giovanni's who died very young of a heart attack. It was a heart that Eugenio had certainly not spared: a big heart, ready to welcome everyone in. One might almost say that Eugenio had died from too much love. But his work went on: the Arcobaleno was an increasingly important presence all over Tuscany.

VI

The district of Santo Spirito lies to the south-east of Florence on the slopes of Boboli. The hill and the city walls together had been decisive in keeping the Oltrarno together, preventing it from being swept up in the chaos of the nineteenth and twentieth-century constructions. The soul of Santo Spirito had been saved, encapsulated between the Arno, the hill of Boboli and the ancient walls that girdle it practically intact from Porta Romana to Porta San Frediano and the tower of Santa Rosa, also on the banks of the Arno.

Eleonora arrived from Naples, although she was Spanish by birth. She was beautiful, with a solemn beauty, an open countenance and a pure gaze, softly-spoken. She arrived in Florence at the age of seventeen to marry Cosimo. Guelfo knew her well. Even before encountering her in the history books, he had been struck by her portrait by Bronzino displayed in Buontalenti's Tribuna in the Uffizi. In it Eleonora appears abstracted, as if she were aware of giving life to a dynasty with her eleven Medici offspring. To one side is the portrait of her infant son Giovanni, laughing and holding a little bird in his hand, blissfully unaware of this weighty destiny. But in Eleonora's large, somewhat soulful eyes, so similar to those of her husband, we can read the determination of one who is aware of making history.

Eleonora was extremely wealthy by birth. This is why it was she, in 1549, who for the price of nine thousand florins purchased the mansion from Bonaccorso Pitti, descendant of Luca Pitti, bringing full circle a story that had begun a hundred years earlier. During the last years of his life Brunelleschi had designed a magnificent new palazzo for the Medici family, which was to stand opposite the church of San Lorenzo, on a site cleared by the demolition of several houses. Cosimo il Vecchio, a prudent man, rejected it since he did not wish to attract the envy of the Florentines. He preferred the more austere palazzo designed by Michelozzo in Via Larga. Luca Pitti did not miss his chance. He purchased the drawings for the palazzo and a few years later entrusted the construction to Brunelleschi's pupil, Luca Fancelli. When the building of the palazzo began in 1458, Luca Pitti was Gonfalonier of Justice. As Niccolò Machiavelli recounted years later in his book *History of Florence and of the Affairs of Italy*:

> The Signoria and Cosimo made lavish presents to Messer Luca, and all the citizens competed in imitation of them, so that it was believed that the money given amounted to no less a sum than twenty thousand ducats. He thus attained such influence, that it was not Cosimo but Messer Luca who now governed the city. And his pride so increased, that he commenced two superb buildings, one in Florence, the other at Ruciano, about a mile distant, larger than any ever built before by a private citizen. To complete them, he had recourse to the most extraordinary means; for not only citizens and private individuals made him presents and supplied materials, but even the ordinary people of the city contributed.
>
> Besides this, any exiles and those who had committed murders, thefts, or other crimes which made them susceptible to public punishment, found a safe refuge within their walls, if they were able to contribute toward their construction.

The Pitti faction was called the hill party, as opposed to that of the Medici in the plain, in Via Larga. But defeat lead to reversal in the fortunes of the Pitti family, and the construction of the palazzo dragged on slowly until it was purchased by Eleonora. Thinking of her many children, the Duchess immediately imagined spacious gardens, and the design was entrusted to Niccolò Pericoli, an anxious genius who was duly nicknamed "Tribolo" (tribulation). While Ammannati set his hand to the design of the magnificent courtyard – which is his masterpiece along with the Ponte Santa Trinita it too built with the hard brown stone from the quarries of Boboli – on 12 May 1549 the Pitti orchard began to be levelled to create what was the very first Italian garden, and one of the most beautiful.

Francesca had been brought up in the Boboli gardens, starting when she was a few months old and Laura would walk her there in her pram. She went in by the Annalena Gate in Via Romana, just a few yards from home, and would then go to the hemicycle on the southern side of the garden, which was where the mothers and children used to meet. In the winter, when it was too cold and windy on the lawns, they would meet at the more sheltered Oceanus fountain. Francesca had practically grown up there, in that fantastic world, so perfect for the eyes and the imagination of a child. What a privilege to have this paradise right on your doorstep! A garden with statues of gods and fauns and nymphs, lions, dogs and eagles, with water plays, mazes of box and laurel hedges, the huge amphitheatre, the Grotto of Buontalenti with Michelangelo's statues of prisoners. Then there were the changing colours of the gardens over the seasons, with the explosion of millions of flowers in the spring and the smell of burning leaves rising from lazy columns of smoke in the autumn. Playing at hide-and-seek became an enchanted journey.

Francesca proudly considered herself a Boboli girl. As she grew older she would even go there alone, certain as she was to meet some friend. When she was about eight or nine she was allowed to explore it on her own, out of sight of Laura, who would remain sitting on a bench chatting to her friends. Running fast, in just a few minutes she'd get as far as the upper gate leading to the Forte Belvedere, along the uphill path that skirted the art Institute and the Bobolino garden. Then down again, past the Kaffeehaus, the Neptune Fountain and the amphitheatre, and a breathless gallop past the Palazzo della Meridiana and the vast Orangery. She'd get back completely out of breath, trying to go as fast as the boys. She would tell Guelfo about it proudly, 'You don't know what you missed!' He would try to replicate with his Piazza d'Azeglio, which was certainly very attractive, but even he realised that there was no comparison. One day Francesca told him about a sort of test that was a ritual in the local district, which had to be performed around the age of sixteen. The idea was to spend the night in the garden, hiding inside at closing time so that you would be locked in. It was a sort of initiation rite that they boys were willing to undergo, whereas very few girls attempted it.

'So, don't tell me, you did it!'

'Of course! What did you expect. And I was only fifteen.'

'OK. So I'll do it too!'

'But you're eighteen! Big deal!'

'Well, that's not my fault. If you've done it I want to do it too; it's important for me.'

They chose the night of the summer solstice, the 21 June. They were getting ready for the school-leaving exam and they were studying together. They entered the garden late, shortly before closing time. When the loudspeaker invited visitors to head towards the gates, Francesca gave Guelfo a kiss and turned to go:

'Right. Be careful, don't get caught. Have you got everything?'

'Sure. Don't worry, I have everything here in my knapsack. Water. Two sandwiches, a sheet, a torch and the poems of Catullus. Ciao!'

'Listen, at midnight go to the statue of *Abundance*, the huge one where she's holding a bunch of wheat. I'll think hard about you and try to imagine where you are. Remember to make a wish!'

'OK. We'll think of each other at midnight. But where will you be?'

'Where do you think? I'll be at home studying.'

Francesca left and Guelfo hid himself in some thick bushes. The first hours, while there was till light, were the most dangerous. He heard the voices of the keepers, chasing up the stragglers, and the clanging of the gardeners' tools as they put them away for the night. Then, finally, all was silence. He watched the sun set on Florence, at that magical hour when the swallows and the bats seem to be fighting for possession of the sky. He saw the lights of the city come on, and the street lamps along the Lungarni. He saw the night gradually taking over the horizon. The large garden came to life. The fireflies invaded the avenues and the lawns, the birds settled themselves in the trees. After a while, as soon as his eyes became accustomed to the darkness, Guelfo could even see the cats chasing each other or hunting. A light breeze rustled the leaves, and the trees sang their eternal song. The fragrances became stronger, and the white marble of the statues stood out clearly against the dark mass of the vegetation.

With his head full of the classical culture that he had thrown himself into body and soul over the last few months of school, Guelfo wandered through the garden as in a dream. All caution and all fear had disappeared. No-one could possibly see him, except perhaps Ceres or Proserpina or Apollo. Indeed he wouldn't have been surprised if they had left their stone prisons for a while and come towards him. Moonlight drenched the thick roots and sinews of the great trees, bathing them in a pale, dense, oily light. They looked like the legs of huge insects, magnified millions of times. Time passed quickly, or perhaps it had stopped:

it truly felt like a time out of time, quite distinct from the almost five centuries of the garden's life. It was a time that had come down from Olympus, the time of Chronos, which had come down to Guelfo through the hundreds of generations of men who had gone before. It was the time of the Veda that continued in circles, immutable and eternal. A time you could listen to and hear it pass, through which you could travel at will backwards and forwards through the centuries. The emotions, the feelings and the hopes of those first men – Egyptians, Indians, Greeks, Romans – were the same as his own.

If it hadn't been for the fact that Francesca was so forcefully present within him, that the thought of her dwelt in him and filled him completely, he would have forgotten about midnight. Instead, at precisely the appointed time, there he was at the feet of the huge statue offering wealth and plenty to the world. He turned to look at the basin below, with the statue of Neptune. Lower down he could make out the slender stele of the obelisk from the Temple of Amun in Thebes, illustrating the exploits of the pharaoh Rameses II in 1500 BC. And beyond, the huge sleeping pile of Palazzo Pitti. Leaping over it in his imagination, just a few hundred metres beyond in the same direction was Francesca's house. He concentrated intensely, closed his eyes and made his wish. 'Francesca, darling...', the words had escaped him and he rested his shoulders on the pedestal of the huge statue.

'Here I am, it's me...'. A hand touched his arm lightly, and Francesca was there, beside him. Guelfo wasn't surprised: his wish had been so heartfelt that Francesca simply had to be there. But he was certain that she had in some way doubled, or split. One of her was at home, sitting with her books at the big walnut table, thinking of him; the other – her image, her soul – had rushed here to his side at his call. Francesca must have read something of this in his dazed look. 'Hey!', id , 'it's me in flesh and blood. You see now that is a magic place!'

But... how did you get in?'

'I'm a Boboli girl, remember? And this is my home. Come on.'

She led him to a little clearing with a huge Lebanon cedar in the middle, its branches almost touching the ground. They curled up together underneath the tree, next to each other, inside each other, indivisible. When Francesca felt Guelfo enter her, without pain, without fear, she realised that she was finally satisfied, replete. She had become a complete human being, with every emptiness filled, including her mother's abandonment. She felt whole, intact, as if when Guelfo penetrated her he had passed right through her body and had driven it into the ground, and her body had sprouted roots. These roots would then develop and grow in all her dealings with men and with sex, and they signified the gift and the sentence of being wife and mother. They signified obedience to the rhythms of life, of the seasons and of the tides, the Sun and the Moon, sowing and harvest. And she knew that every time she attempted to escape this destiny she would suffer and would lose her way. It was she who had decided everything: when, where, how. Who knows what sort of ancestral instinct she was obeying: something unwritten, uncodified and for that very reason even more sacred and immutable. But she'd felt certain that this nascent love she felt for Guelfo was a strong sentiment. She was also more than certain that love, sex and procreation were the female domain: a magical labyrinth through which men had to be guided, taken by the hand. They were like clumsy children, ever prone to make a wrong move, to say too much, uttering a word that would break the spell. What endless havoc they'd caused, these preposterous warriors, these knights of the absurd, in pursuit of their elusive fortune! How many times had Francesca thought about the Greek heroes of her beloved mythology, the disasters wrought by these sentimental illiterates, leaving in their wake a trail of grieving women, driven to madness or suicide or transformed into simulacra. No, love was far too important a matter to be left in the hands of men.

At the moment of orgasm Guelfo immediately sensed that death had been vanquished. All deaths redeemed. He realised that Lorenzo continued to live with him, within Francesca. They fell asleep and awoke with the first light of dawn. Francesca led him out of the garden; sure of her way, they climbed up a wall and clambered over an iron grating. Then they walked towards Piazza Santo Spirito. In Via dei Serragli Francesca knocked on the door of Masi the baker and got them to give her some freshly-baked bread, still warm.

'Francesca, what on earth are you doing out and about at this time of day?' asked the baker.

Guelfo replied: 'We've been up studying all night, and we got hungry...'

But Francesca interrupted him, 'No, that's not true. We've been making love.... but the hunger bit is true!'

'And quite right too, I say,' replied the baker, 'you're a lovely couple and if you don't make love at your age, I don't know who should. Take the bread as a gift from me.'

They left the baker's and Francesca put her arm round Guelfo's waist, biting into the warm bread. 'I don't want to lie,' she said, 'especially about something so wonderful!'

'You're right,' agreed Guelfo, 'never again, I swear!' he too took a bite, and the fragrance of the warm bread wafted around them like a cloud.

VII

Guelfo decided to turn on the light. It was almost four o'clock, but it seemed as though he'd given up any idea of sleeping that night. Unlike Balthazar, who in the meantime had curled up happily in an armchair and was snoring peacefully. Anyway, tomorrow was Saturday, and he had nothing special to do. He hadn't been mistaken. With the light on, the apartment was exactly the way he remembered it. Francesca had made a point of not changing anything, leaving everything exactly as it was. Only the fresh flowers in the vases had been replaced with huge bunches of artificial silk flowers.

It felt as though the people living in the house had just popped out and would be returning any minute. The living and the dead. Or perhaps they had never left. Guelfo could clearly see Giovanni, wearing one of his loose cardigans, brown corduroy trousers and suede shoes, searching the shelves in the library for a book he wanted to show him. The music was missing. That wonderful music that spoke of love that he'd heard there for the first time: Jacques Brel, Chico Buarque, Gino Paoli, Edith Piaf and Tom Jobim. And the great jazz of Miles Davis, John Coltrane, Charlie Parker and Billie Holiday.

The school finals had gone well. Francesca's full marks came as no surprise, and it was no more than she deserved. He too had been very satisfied with his own mark of 54 out of 60, which would have been unimaginable a couple of months earlier. It was all thanks to Francesca, with her everything became easy.

He had felt as though he were walking five feet off the ground. He had so much energy that if he had fallen he would have bounced up again like a ball. Even at basketball he'd never played so well. They'd prepared for their exams together. When he'd been called for his oral, Francesca's admonition, 'Go and show them what you're made of!' had been enough to make him give of his best.

At university they'd both gone for the Faculty of Letters: Francesca to study Art History and Guelfo Mediaeval History. Giovanni had been instrumental in helping him to make this decision.

'Guelfo, studying is a privilege. The brain is a muscle just like others and if it's not used, it atrophies. It's true that your parents have a thriving business, but if you want to be a historian you shouldn't be put off. It's a wonderful profession, which will enrich you with knowledge if not with money. In any case you already have money, so you don't need to worry.'

Now that he had more time, Guelfo had been able to devote himself to reading all the books he'd never read, distracted as he had always been by the computer. Giovanni would enthusiastically select his reading:

'You don't know how lucky you are to have all this treasure still to be discovered. Although you have to remember that it's not the quantity that counts. Ovid had only eighty volumes in his library; it was incredible at the time, but only what you'd find in practically any home today, or rather what you would have found up to a few years ago. And yet he was Ovid! When push comes to shove, there are only a few dozen really important books, even for people like me who've read thousands.'

And so Guelfo had experienced the overweening ambition of Julien Sorel, Captain Ahab's desperate challenge to God, the cynicism of George Duroy. He shared the infinite patience of Florentino Ariza as he waited for Fermina Dasa, the tremulous passion of Professor Aschenbach for the young Tadzio, the magical world of the Buendia and their women, Ursula, Amaranta, Remedios. He was Connie Chatterley being opened to life by

Oliver Mellors. He descended to the depths of the tormented soul of Ivan Karamazov, found refuge in the welcoming world of David Copperfield and the placid strength of Mrs. Ramsey. He relived the clear-sighted and disenchanted agony of the Prince of Salina, and Concetta's incurable bitterness. He waltzed with Natasha Rostov, was at Borodino with Andrei and dragged the body of Marius through the sewers of Paris with Jean Valjean. He alighted from the train with Anna going to meet her inevitable fate. He was on the saddle of Vronsky's horse in the tragic steeplechase, and was imprisoned in Parma with Fabrice del Dongo. With Ida's failing strength he vainly defended the lives of Nino and Useppe. He sailed on the *Pequod* and on the *Narcissus*. He blended into the everyday stories of the poor folk of Via del Corno. He destroyed with Emma Bovary and built with Kitty and Konstantin Levin. He betrayed Swann and loved Odette.

And at night, exhausted, after he closed the book and switched off the light, he frequently remained suspended in their world. These intriguing and eternal characters were like friends who entered your imagination and yourlife never to leave it again. One of the things that Guelfo and Francesca loved best was to stay in bed, each with their own books, their legs entwined, reading the best bits aloud to each other as they came to them. Accompanied by a jar of Nutella, and making love whenever they felt like it. Especially after Guelfo moved into his own apartment, they would spent days at a time in this way. Judging by the results, it was apparently conducive to study.

It was always exciting talking to Giovanni about books. To explain to Guelfo the importance he attributed to them, he had shown him the letter sent by Cardinal Bessarion to the Doge Cristoforo Moro on 31

May 1468, when he donated to Venice his library of 482 Greek texts and 264 in Latin.

> Books are full of the words of sages, the example of the ancients, customs, laws and religion. They live, discourse and speak to us, they teach us, they train us, they console us and show us, placing the most distant things in our memory before our eyes. So great is their dignity, their majesty and, finally, their sanctity that, if it were not for books we would all be rude and ignorant, without any memory of the past, without any example. We would have no knowledge of any thing, human or divine, and the very urn that holds the ashes would cancel the very memory of men.

Giovanni explained to him the historic context within which any given masterpiece saw the light. He probed the writings and the psychology of the writer and the characters, bringing out the unknown and obscure side, illuminating the creative process. He also talked about cinema and about how it had changed. Up to a few years ago, there had been cinemas everywhere. Now, with the huge TV screens in every home, people went less and less frequently and the cinemas were disappearing. Cable TV allowed you to choose what film you wanted to watch – the latest release or one from fifty years ago. You simply had to request it and pay for it, just like an old juke box. On Giovanni's advice Guelfo had watched De Sica and Rossellini, Visconti and Fellini, Bergman, Truffaut, Billy Wilder, Woody Allen and many others: a magnificent feast of cinema.

'So you can make a film without special effects. With people who talk like ordinary people and that ordinary things happen to? I didn't think that was possible,' he said to Giovanni.

'You bet it was possible, Guelfo,' replied Giovanni, 'and being in the cinema, everyone together in the dark theatre, it was even better. Going to see a good film with a friend, and then a pizza afterwards, was one of the nicest ways of spending an evening.'

Then Francesca would tease Giovanni for his nostalgia.

'Listen to you! You could have written *À la recherche du temps perdu* yourself, our Proust of Santo Spirito.'

'Go on, then! Make fun of me. But even if New York hadn't been blown to bits, you'd have had to be blind not to see what was happening. That we were entering into another Barbarian age. The twentieth century was totally devastating. It destroyed all balance, broke down every barrier: ecological, demographic and moral. I was already saying these things when I was your age, when very few people thought that way. Everyone was captivated by the wealth and progress that for the first time was being doled out in abundance, to all social classes. It seemed as though the process would never end, a Biblical manna guaranteed by omnipotent science and technology. From one billion the population burgeoned to seven billion. The countryside was abandoned. Many huge cities with over ten million inhabitants sprang up: abnormal monsters, excrescences on the face of the earth. At the same time, in the space of just a few years, you could no longer bathe in the sea or in a river. We were forced to drink only mineral water. The air that we breathed was seriously polluted; sunbathing was sure to lead to cancer. We destroyed all the forests, caused the extinction of almost all the animals, including the large mammals, which live on like sad ghosts of their former selves only in a handful of zoos or in kids' cartoons.

We've lost all confidence in our hands, which hardly anyone knows how to use any more, or is anyway ashamed to admit it. We've invented this artificial and fictitious life for ourselves, with absurd values – or, rather, no values at all. In order to be freer to do what we want and indulge our search for pleasure we've transformed the unreal into the real, and then believed in it. We have reduced entire continents into a situation of meaningless misery, robbing them of their culture and imposing on them a destructive and hostile model of life, depriving them of all dignity. Man has made a desert of his heart and his conscience. And all for white goods, TVs, cars and mobile phones, for cupboards crammed with god knows what, for skiing holidays and New Year in the Maldives. The huge glut of objects has throttled our souls.

And then we have to add to these poisoned gifts the chance for women to have children at any age, or even through a surrogate mother, perhaps to offset the fact that most women no longer manage to become mothers. They become depressed and desperate at the thought of having in their womb or in their arms a creature who needs their total attention, that can't be turned on or off at the flick of a switch.

No, there can be no pardon for the twentieth century: the century that ushered in total war, mass extermination, the atom bomb. Despite the undeniable progress made in medicine, physics and space research, the price paid was too high, and progress without ethics proved ephemeral. Small wonder then that great art abandoned it before it was even half-way through, except for the rarest exceptions. And yet nowadays dozens of millions of people have the chance to study the arts in schools and academies and universities, in the vast array of courses on offer all over the world: never before has study and training been so widely available. And yet, despite that, painting and music are dead. The man of today, the man spawned by the twentieth century, has lost his way. True art has always had the task of trailblazer, of showing the path to the rest of mankind. But now no-one knows where to go. When humanity gets out of this impasse – if it gets out – art will return to performing its task. For the present, it's in hibernation, and this sleep has lasted for more than seventy years. If the sacrifice of New York serves to change all this, becomes the epitaph of barbarianism and the forceps of a new era, it will not have been in vain.'

Giovanni would get very worked up at such times, and would completely lose his habitual smiling and slightly sad air of well-disposed wisdom. It was because he'd been through too much and he was exhausted by all this idiocy. Since he was very young he'd seen what was happening and had spoken out against it. He'd engaged in struggles for civil rights, animal rights and for the protection of nature. He'd countered on every front the vision of the material world that reigned supreme, hurtling forward without compass and without brakes. With a few friends of his he'd founded a journal, which for years had sought to open people's eyes to the looming disaster.

During the years when John Paul II was Pope he'd believed that something might change. He, an atheist, was full of admiration for this Polish Pope who had started his pontificate with the cry "DO NOT BE AFRAID!" ringing out in Saint Peter's Square, striking the whole world. What he meant was: do not be afraid to be Christians, do not be afraid to make sacrifices, to do without, do not be afraid to have hope. Open the doors wide for Christ. Christ knows "what is in man". He alone knows it. This cry had swept away in an instant the pathetic whisperings of so many of the recent Italian Popes, the hesitant voices, the measured words, what was said and what was left unsaid. No. This Pope shouted, exhorted, threatened, urged. He was a strong man in the ancient mould, invoking God: a fiery God, Lord of the cosmos, with a thunder bolt in his fist. He was a Pope prepared to fight the devil, whose presence he saw oppressing the world. He had held up the Cross before a benighted society. Like Saint Paul, he preached the language of the Cross, stubbornly, bringing it to every corner of the world. It was a terrible admonition of the evident impossibility of man to realise his destiny without God.

For the Jubilee of 2000 Giovanni and his friends had walked to Rome, along the footpaths of the ancient pilgrims' route, the Via Francigena. It was an act of devotion and respect for the old Pope, a pilgrimage that confirmed their feeling as a People of God, believers or non-believers, Christians in any case by birth and belonging. It had been a wonderful experience. It had taken them about ten days, with two donkeys to carry their rucksacks, and one of them who had difficulty walking. When they finally saw it in the distance, Giovanni realised that Rome was the most important city that had ever existed in the world: the authentic Eternal City. Over the course of history many peoples had dominated, and if their greatness was to be judged by what they had left behind, by their contribution to universal civilisation, there could be no doubt that the role of Rome was peerless. Even now it was still the centre of Christendom, after having given man law, language and countless other gifts.

But Wojtyla too had passed on, had been defeated. He who had put an end to Communism on his own, twenty years ahead of time, had had to surrender: to a calibre 9 bullet, to old age, to weariness, but above all to a world that didn't want rules, that didn't want bridles, that every day added more to the weighty burden of its demands. A society of individuals all devoted to gratifying their own selfishness, without giving up anything: good-for-nothings who would stop at nothing. Despite the innumerable warning signs, they wanted it all, and they wanted it now, in a pig-headed desire for self-destruction.

And so we had homosexual marriage, pensions at age forty, shops open round the clock, children at any age and by any means, genetic aberrations, cloning. Even though there were laws prohibiting the latter, but there was always ways round them. You just had to pay. Hollywood was launching clones of the old stars, raised in concealment and cynically thrown onto the set. Many of the rich and powerful could not resist the idea of rearing their own junior doubles.

'We have to save the word,' Giovanni would never tire of repeating, 'and with the word the emotions it expresses, our humanity. The last bastion of the word is paper – books – just as it used to be the clay tablet.' This was his great battle. He held conferences and wrote articles to save the printed word from the invasion of the video, the computer or the television, whatever it might be. He had founded an association for the purpose. He considered that the generation of Francesca and Guelfo was seriously at risk, and that the formative power of the video had not yet been entirely understood. He felt that, although it was so widely employed, to date video had been used mostly by people who had been educated through the written word. But the younger generation had been accustomed to computers since primary school, and to a teaching based much more on the image than on the word. They had been subject to the sensory bombardment of the video and were being transformed into a different kind of being, with a different brain and a new and unknown perception of reality and the world.

For Giovanni, the library continued to be the fulcrum of thought. In his studies he returned to the time in which emotions and feelings were transmitted first by sounds and only much later through words. He was trying to save the beautiful and rich world of the oral tradition. He had a passionate interest in cultural anthropology; he adored Lévi-Strauss, and thought that it was a tragedy for civilisation not to pass down the words. It was an emotional impoverishment, a stark loss of freedom and a condemnation to the loss of memory.

'So,' said Guelfo,' to get on well in life, all you need is a good library?'

'It's not quite as simple as that, and above all it's not that easy,' replied Giovanni. 'It's not as if you decide how to live after having read a few books, or even lots of books. It doesn't work like that. You live, full stop.'

Giovanni always recommended reading in the open air, in the midst of nature, letting the wind, the leaves, the clouds, the smell of the sea and the rays of the sun pass through the pages. Casting the ideas around, bringing them to life, confusing them, in the eternal exchange between nature and thought that underlies everything. It was the only possible mirror of God. Years later, following Giovanni's ideas, Guelfo would get his students on the university course to copy old fifteenth-century books. Precise copies of the originals which the students would make using quill pens and ink. The students were very struck by this extraordinary procedure. But they never forgot it again, and they succeeded in understanding the importance of those old texts which had come down to them through the centuries. In just a few years the department had a fine library. All the volumes were bound in leather by the students themselves under the watchful eye of an old craftsman bookbinder, Armando, who had taught them this ancient art. It was always a moving moment when, at the end, the title would be engraved on the cover in gold letters.

Poliphili Hypnerotomachia, ubi humana omnia non nisi somnium esse ostendit, atque obiter plurima scitu quam digna commemorat

Victoria Buffi fecit - Firenze 2026

["Poliphilo's *Strife of Love in a Dream*, wherein he shows that all human things are but a dream and in which many things are deemed worthy of remembrance." The tale is by the Renaissance humanist Francesco Colonna]

VIII

One day, Guelfo decided it was his turn to ask Giovanni a question.

'May I, sir?'

'Of course, go ahead.'

'Laura'.

Giovanni remained in silence for a moment, then replied, 'Laura, what? Laura why?'

'Because you know everything about me: I've told you things I didn't even have the courage to tell myself, things I didn't even know. But as far as you, sir, and Francesca are concerned, I know practically nothing about this aspect of your lives that I sense is extremely important. And I get the impression that Francesca doesn't want to talk about it.'

Giovanni settled better into his chair, turned it towards Guelfo and then stretched out his legs and crossed them. He put on a thoughtful expression, almost comical, and scratched his head.

'Listen Guelfo... first of all let's drop the formalities; I can't tell my life story to someone who's calling me sir.'

Guelfo nodded without interrupting.

'How many things have we talked about over these two years that you've been hanging around here? As well as about you and your family, I mean. We've talked about poetry and music, about literature and politics, about the cinema, about morality and religion. It's all wonderful, it's all fascinating. But...,' Giovanni stopped, as if gathering his thoughts.

'But what?' insisted Guelfo.

'But... there's nothing like a woman, believe me! Ok. Think about all those great classics that you're

reading, about the films we've seen. What intr
most? What's the first thing that comes to m
na Karenina, Rossella O'Hara, Margherita G
And the same happens in real life. I've never ˍˍˍ ın
war but perhaps – so distant, so different – it may be
the only thing that resembles a great love. In terms of
intensity, pathos, totality, and influence on fate. And
then when you have love and war together, love and
death, then that's the absolute pinnacle. Laura was the
love of my life, that's for sure, and for that I'll always
be grateful to her. She gave value to my life, she allowed me to feel things that I didn't even know existed before. I can't imagine what my life would have been
like without her. And now, over more than six years
since she left, you couldn't exactly say that I'm doing
fine. I'm hesitant about living. Or, rather, only a part
of me is alive, the other part has been amputated. It's
strange in a way, because in all the years we were together, I also felt a certain nostalgia for my freedom.
Things were fine between us, at least on my side, but
the thought of not being able to fall in love again sad
dened me.

I don't mean sex, don't get me wrong. In love,
what's really important is the discovery, the encounter,
the excitement of knowing another person. Everything
that you simply imagine when you see a face passing
on the street, a glance that remains fixed in your mind's
eye. The dream mechanism triggered by a smile, by
the gesture of an arm or the way of tossing the head
and hair. And that sets off something inside you, shiv-
ers through every fibre of your being, hits you in the
guts and ends up lapping at your heart. That's the magic, and it's unique every time.

The secret of seduction lies in striking the imagination of the other person. The great seducers are men
whose feminine side is highly developed. Managing to
strike the object of desire in such a way that they think
that with him – or with her – everything will be differ-

ent. And often you don't even ask yourself whether the change will be for better or for worse. We're all ready to run the risk in this great adventure. It's something deeply rooted inside us. Sex is another matter. It's a much more direct, more primitive instinct. Of course it's important, but not as important as it's made out to be. As I see it, even Freud fell into that trap: a scientist of the nineteenth century, we mustn't forget, who started out by cutting the brain into thin slices, trying to find the traces of neuroses, of disease. He needed "material", and sexuality and libido was the only thing that could supply it.'

Giovanni was off. He twisted in his chair, jumped to his feet, paced nervously around the room. Who knows how long he'd been needing to get all this stuff about Laura off his chest.

'I can't stand these confused memories any longer, this overlaying of images, this emotional short-circuit!'

Guelfo sat still and silent. He was both curious and startled at having opened the floodgates to this outpour.

'And to think that I always kept other lives in reserve, as if the one I was living was not enough. I've done it since I was a child. Even with Laura, and Francesca. Even when I was totally happy. I'd say to myself: if they weren't around I could go round the world in a boat, facing new challenges, having adventures, meeting new people. But when Laura left these defences simply didn't work. Dreams, especially those you have nurtured at length, have to stay dreams. Otherwise they unravel; like old lace kept under glass that turns to dust on contact with the air. I tried to invent new ones, but they refused to take shape. It was as if my creative imagination, which had always been almost uncontrollably fertile, had been clogged up. Now it works only for Francesca. For her I can imagine the future, different situations and achievements. I can't do it for me. Laura has dried up a large part of me, even my imagination. O rather it's that my imagination continues to pursue her, obsessively, in every thought, every moment. And then the heart... the heart.

For years now I've been living in two time zones: mine and Laura's. I even wear two watches. I know her schedules, her habits. I can imagine where she is at every moment: when she leaves home, when she goes to the beach or to the office, when she reads the paper or listens to music or does gym. Since I don't want to phone her, I call when I know she's out, just so I can hear her voice on the answering machine. And me – who's always hated the phone – I rush to answer it, always hoping that it might be her calling to speak to Francesca. Just to steal a couple of words, exchange a few pleasantries: the tyrant Love! When Laura left I cried for months, starting in the shower every morning, mingling drops of water and pain. A dull, pervasive pain that the few hours of sleep I managed to wrest from sleeping pills didn't minimally affect, and that I found again every morning at the foot of the bed, obstinate and faithful like a pair of old slippers. What could I do? Look for someone else? And how could I burden them with all that weight? How would they have been able to stand it? No. It was too late; maybe if had happened ten years earlier it might have worked, but how could I forget or replace fifteen years of my life?

I tried to get back into making love, very slowly and very fearfully. All the bodies seemed hard to me, closed in armour, impenetrable even as I penetrated them. When they were younger girls they seemed to me like bodies without history, their smooth flesh like plastic, without memory. I felt totally extraneous. In the first few years I went on trying; I even had a few love affairs, or attempted to. My self-esteem was flattered by the advances of interesting older ladies. But it couldn't work. I understand now that I cannot be so intimate with a stranger as to kiss them. A shag maybe, even desire sometimes, but as for any other form of intimacy

– such as a kiss – I don't feel like sharing that with anyone. Every so often I masturbate; in fact it's something I've always done, in every period of my life. Apart from that, I have my good days and my bad days, which is par for the course for a troubled soul like me. The truth is that I keep myself free, alone, available, in the eternal hope that Laura may come back. Because I know now that the much-praised freedom has no value at all in itself. Your freedom only becomes inestimably precious when you consciously make a gift of it to someone: when you're happy to relinquish it for the love of a person, or an idea.

Sometimes I comfort myself with the notion that she left me so that I would love her for ever, to ensure that my destiny was accomplished. That she did it as the ultimate test of this absolute love, finally freed from the paltry dailiness, accounts to be paid, reciprocal selfishness, jealousy. The person who leaves, who disappears – like someone who dies, or even more so – is taken by the Gods to their Olympus. You can't have everything. Our very meeting, that moment of such intense passion, already contained the certainty of the end. Like Tristan and Isolde. You can't have Isolde married and turned plump several years later going round the supermarket with a trolley, buying groceries and saving up the stamps for a free dinner service. And so we won't have the chance of growing old together. We won't spend the evenings watching some old film on the TV, or sitting in armchairs, each with his or her book, the silence interrupted only by the banal sounds of the dog scratching itself or a car passing in the distance, the next-door neighbour. When, behind the page you're reading, you sense the presence of that other person: close, friendly, your safe harbour by ingrained habit. All the things that you can do together, and that once you've done them together – with that particular person – when you do them alone seem emptied of all meaning, bringing you endlessly back to the song of your solitude.

I live in this absence. Neruda said, "I am absent. /Live in my absence as if in a house." That's what I do. A full house, as you see: too full, especially of her presence. But I miss the daily exchange of little discoveries, intuitions, thoughts; sharing joys and sorrows, fears and surprises. And I can count myself lucky because I have Francesca at my side: the most fantastic person in the world. This being who is still incomplete and yet already so mature, so much a friend, the fruit of my life: the end product of a clear-sighted, loyal and sincere way of life. When I look at her I feel so proud, and –why not? – I even feel proud of myself.'

Giovanni smiled, he relaxed into his chair and passed his hand over his forehead and his eyes, almost as if to banish the crowding thoughts.

'Well, I don't think I've said anything new. The subject of love has filled numerous libraries. Even in times like this, when love is out of fashion, has been disembowelled in every possible way. It's just that this is my story, my experience: banal if compared to that of humanity, but totally unique and special for me.'

Guelfo didn't look at him. He kept his head lowered, as if this confession had embarrassed him. He felt like an intruder in someone else's world. Giovanni turned his back on him and began to busy himself with his papers and drawers: a clock that didn't work, an invitation to a show, a letter from a friend.

'Do you think… forgive me, but do you think that, between me and Francesca it could last for ever?' Guelfo's voice sounded like a supplication. It was like the voice of a small child, so great was the hope in it, the yearning for confirmation. Giovanni, who was still stirred by his own outburst, by the crowding memories, was moved by it. He swivelled round and rolled his chair closer to Guelfo's, so close that their knees almost touched. He took Guelfo's hands and he squeezed them tight.

'My dear, dear boy. Who knows? Who can say? Live these days, these years, in happiness and don't torment yourself. You make such a fine pair: when you come into the house it's like a breath of spring. When I hear you running down the stairs, I go to the window to watch you crossing the square. I look out and I see it filled with your youth. It's like a fragrance that rises up the walls of the buildings and enters people's homes, their lives. It's a fragrance that makes the bells ring, makes the dogs bark, makes the trees dance. Banks lower the interest rates for your love, and shopkeepers give their goods away free. That fat widow will invite the milkman's wife to dinner, and a stray cat will find a new home. For your love, Guelfo, only for your love. It's a miracle: your own special miracle. Don't ask how long it will last.'

IX

It had lasted almost another three years: three wonderful years, when everything went smoothly. In Francesca's room Guelfo could see some photos from that time. Their graduation ceremonies. The two of them on Ponza nine years earlier. On horseback at Les Saintes Maries de la Mer, where they had felt so proud to learn that the Camargue and its nature park had been created through the initiative of a Florentine, Marquis Baroncelli. Here they were again, having breakfast in a bar in Saint Germain, and there in a boat on the Serpentine in Hyde Park, surrounded by ducks. They were smiling and happy, in those overflowing moments when you sense that your only home is life, and youth. Despite everything elsc, despite the world that was wearily attempting to get back on its feet after the catastrophe that had struck it.

Then one day it was all over, suddenly, just like that. Francesca had been in Paris for three months doing an intern at UNESCO. When she came back she told Guelfo in the space of a few minutes, releasing herself from his embrace.

'Guelfo, they've offered me a scholarship for two years, and I've decided to accept it. I'm really sorry, believe me, but I know it's the right thing to do. I just know it, I feel it.'

'But Paris is just three hours away by train, it doesn't mean anything...'

'Yes it does. It means everything. It means that it's all over between us.' Francesca's voice droned in Guelfo's ears like a tired hornet.

'Over, over... what's over? Can breathing, drinking, walking be over?'

Thinking about it years later, Guelfo continued to be amazed at the way women managed to bring their love affairs to such an abrupt end. He heard his own voice saying,

'For God's sake Francesca cut it out! You're hurting me...'

'And how do you think I feel? I know exactly how you're feeling because I feel exactly the same. We have to learn to live on our own. We've been together for so long, we grew up together, so that it seems impossible that it could be any other way. We've built a past for ourselves, memories. When first met we were two puppies, we take our leave of each other as grown-up people: good people, strong and willing. What good luck we had to travel so much road together, and what fun it was! And you don't even think a thing like that's worth suffering for? Isn't it worth a bit of pain? Don't put the whole burden, all the responsibility on me. If you want I can take it for both of us, but it's not fair. You should be ashamed of yourself.'

As usual, Francesca had been better-prepared and more courageous than he was. In an instant she had resolved all the doubts, the moods and the discomfort that they'd been suffering from for several months.

'Guelfo, that's the way it is and you know it. We have been over-indulgent and even stupid not to admit it before. Our time's up and there's nothing more to be done. The more we put it off, analyse or ignore it, the more we'll get bogged down and hurt ourselves. Just think about us recently. It never used to happen that we argued, tolerated each other or bored each other! No, it's over now. If we were supposed to spend our whole lives together it wouldn't have happened. We didn't want it, we didn't choose it. Apparently it's our destiny and we just have to accept it. I can't imagine anyone better than you, and I would have given anything for it to last for ever.'

Guelfo had tried to protest, but as he did so he re-alised how right Francesca was. It was as though a boulder had been removed from his heart, and yet it suffered – boy, how it suffered! Imagining all the future days without Francesca – her phone call that woke him up in the early morning, or the way she'd come home, opening the door with her own keys and jump into bed beside him fully-dressed – wasn't just painful, it was impossible.

They'd continued to see each other regularly, as friends, in the weeks leading up to Francesca's departure. The atmosphere was a bit forced, always over the top, full of exaggerated cheerfulness and embarrassed silences. When the morning came for Giovanni and him to accompany her to the station, it was almost a relief.

'Giovanni, listen, even if Francesca's gone, I can still come to see you, can't I?'

'You not only can, you must, Guelfo! If you don't find the company of this old boy too heavy-going. Francesca did the right thing. She always does the right thing, damn her! Sometimes it would be better if she didn't. Anyway, no more sadness! Today I'm inviting you to lunch. If we weren't already friends this would be the perfect occasion to quote the last line of *Casablanca*, when Rick says "Louis, I think this is the beginning of a beautiful friendship."' And indeed, left on their own, Guelfo and Giovanni developed an un-expected familiarity. By now they were both adults and the age difference was no longer an issue, although the profound difference in knowledge was. But the transfer proceeded apace, going both ways, because to Giovanni's experience and his vast culture, Guelfo was able to add, and to oppose, the dazzling intuitions of youth. He contributed his curiosity and the pointed questions that would force his older friend to explain, to re-elaborate and question himself, even about things he'd felt sure of. Together they reread Thucydides,

Toynbee, Konrad Lorenz and Ignazio Silone. Giovanni introduced Guelfo to Illich and Pasolini. They spent entire evenings with the great poets, from Homer, Dante, and Shakespeare through to Leopardi, Kafavis, Neruda, Garcia Lorca and Achmatova.

Giovanni read with great passion. He had acted when young and he had the technique which, combined with his fine voice, would reveal the text in all its harmony. He knew the most intriguing anecdotes, like the one about Garcia Lorca's mother who, on her last visit to her son in prison before his execution, let her lipstick slide into his hand as she embraced him for the last time. It meant that she had always known about his homosexuality, which the poet had jealously guarded for fear of paining her, and that she didn't care at all, that she loved him all the more.

Giovanni was also passionate about cooking, which resulted in delicious dinners. Guelfo had to pay the price by running errands hither and thither to procure the strangest ingredients, following Giovanni's precise instructions: it was more like a treasure hunt than shopping.

'Have you got that straight? You go to that particular stall in the market and ask for Piero. Tell him I sent you, he already knows all about it. Be sure you don't go before ten or after eleven. He'll give you a packet. Don't open it. It's already paid for. Bring it to me as quick as you can because I have to prepare it and then leave it to rest.' Guelfo was convinced that one of these days they were going to arrest him as part of who knows what subversive organisation – the Black Truffle Band. What a fine name for a plot! And indeed, Piero, or whoever else it might me, would always immediately abandon their customers or whatever they were doing and take him to one side with a conspiratorial air. Then they would tell him to take it with all haste to Giovanni – or to "the Professor", depending on the degree of intimacy – who had already called and was waiting for him. Then in the evening Guelfo would realise that it might be a Chianina beefsteak, or sausages of Cinta Senese. Or perhaps a bass that had been swimming in the sea off Elba just a few hours before, or a piece of the banned Colonnata lard, or spices from Kurdistan. That's the way Giovanni was. And as he cooked he would declaim poetry that went with the recipe or with the food. He would set up a dialogue – which was inevitably always a monologue – with the sacrificed creature. Sometimes he'd even go so far as to imitate its movements, in a surreal dance.

'Don't laugh! Almost all the ancient peoples did it and the indigenous Americans – the few who have survived – still do it today. If you eat the flesh of the cow, the pig or the sturgeon, then you have to thank them. You have to include them in the gift they're making to you, expressing your gratitude for their sacrifice. It's an ancient custom, from a time when men lived in symbiosis with other animals and respected their souls, a time when the world hung together, harmonious and undivided, as in the time of the Etruscans. Otherwise the animals might have been offended and have left the area, and then the tribe would have died of hunger.'

Publisher friends were always asking him to write a cookery book. But when he started to do it, the first two recipes alone ran to thirty pages. Giovanni would bring together Artusi and Freud, Escoffier and Sesto Caio Baccelli, he would digress into Mayakovsky and could end up with Bach and Cimabue.

'That's the way it is, Guelfo, the preparation of a dish encompasses everything: the earth, history, art, the psychology of the person who makes it and the people who eat it, the seasons, the climate, love. "Take a knob of butter" How does that strike you? Listen to the sound, every bit as fine as "In the beginning was the Word". It has the same solemnity, the same anticipation of something great, something creative. Cooking is creation. I am the demiurge of *Pappa al Po-*

modoro Santo Spirito style. And it's a completely different thing from what they serve on the other side of the Arno. And how could it not be? It's a different territory, with a different history. Here we can already breathe the air of Chianti,' he explained, stretching his neck and nose in the direction of Impruneta. 'The Sienese Crete, Santa Caterina and on good days you can even smell the sea, there beyond Mount Amiata.' At this point Giovanni's neck looked like that of a giraffe and he stretched his whole body upwards standing on tiptoe. 'On the other side of the Arno you feel Mugello, the cold of the Apennines, the great concentration of banks and offices, Osmannoro and the Business District. It's the *Pappa al pomodoro* of the advanced services sector.'

'Hang on, Giovanni, you frequently send me to buy the ingredients at the market of San Lorenzo. Well, isn't that on the other side of the Arno?'

'Exactly, that's why I always tell you to get them back to me quickly, so that I can keep them here, prepare them, civilise them, marry them with our own ingredients and then leave them to rest.'

'Yes and then when they wake up they go to play historic football with the Bianchi of Santo Spirito!' Guelfo burst out laughing, but Giovanni wasn't so easily put down.

'Less of your insolence, my lad. "There are more things in heaven and kitchen, Horatio, / Than are dreamt of in your philosophy."'

In a word, Giovanni's recipe book would have become an encyclopaedia, and so it came to nothing. But it was a shame, because his recipes were fantastic – really fantastic, and reading them was as much a delight for the spirit as eating them was for the taste buds. The guests at these dinners were Giovanni's few friends: the tried and trusted friends of a lifetime, comrades of the streets and the alleys who had shared hopes, money, illusions and loss. They were bound together by ingrained habit, by the many battles they had fought together: all of them lost, but to their greater glory. They were always the few against the many: against everyone, against the world. The numerous political movements they'd been active in or founded had never succeeded in passing the 3% threshold at the time of reckoning of the elections. The print-runs of their newspapers were between one thousand and three thousand copies, most of them left unsold.

'Definitely a highly select aristocracy,' joked Stefano, the most intellectual of the group, son of farming folk.

'An elite, or rather an ethylic, class with all the wine we've drunk,' retorted Fabrizio.

'Actually the definition of aristocracy is spot-on. It has nothing to do with blood or birth. The true aristocrats are those who possess strength and greatness of soul, the capacity for solitude, combined with profound goodness and a total lack of self-interest.'

'In a way it's the lesson of Kant: the moral law that requires that you must do your duty without expecting a reward of any kind.'

'Yes, a lesson trampled on by the French Revolution in just a couple of years. Which led to the endless claims for rights that have never since ceased: sacrosanct at first, then becoming increasingly more absurd.'

Despite everything – the profusion of intellects, engaged conversation, the staggering problems threatening the world that were analysed between one course and the next – the evenings somehow always ended up in hilarious high spirits, convulsive laughter and withering quips. Guelfo enjoyed himself no end at the sight of these irresistible old boys, these diehards, obstinately attached to life, to its Dionysian aspect. So far removed from women, they always ended up talking about women. The departure of Laura had been seen as a loss for the group.

'Where on earth do you find another beauty like that? I only ever saw her at the cinema. I felt about six feet tall just because she spoke to me.'

'Oh Lord, we thank you for having given her to us, not because you took her away.'

Giovanni tried to object, 'Hey lads, have a little respect. You know I don't like this sort of talk.'

'Come off it! What have you got to complain of? In your whole life you'd been with three poor wretches. Waking up every morning for fifteen years with Laura beside you was like winning the pools every day: a bloomin' world record.'

'When Laura realised that there were such things as oculists in the world, she scarpered back to Brazil.'

And if Giovanni got touchy, they could go on like this for hours. But it hardly ever happened. He too liked talking about her.

'Well, so here we are! The upshot of it is that, after all our efforts, we're going to be condemned to die with the microchip. Branded like cattle. A very nice affair!'

'This damned microchip: it's the sign of our infamy, we deserved it!'

'Not us, lads! No, not us! At least we have that to be proud of. We did everything we could. We devoted half our lives to politics, understood in the highest sense, at the service of ideas, of the city. And we paid everything out of our own pockets – posters, newspapers, events and conferences. Thousands of evenings spent in debate. You really begin to wonder why the hell we bothered.'

'We bothered because we wanted to, evidently it was our fate, our nature to do so. I don't regret anything. It's all fine with me. Even the microchip's fine, if that's the price to be paid, if the end justifies the means. We are the heirs of Machiavelli and Guicciardini, and the means certainly shouldn't frighten us. Politics shouldn't frighten us, not real politics, but rather the lack of politics, the empty simulacrum of politics. This is what has led to the disaster: the lack of responsibility – that of society and of each individual – the loss of a moral sense, of dignity. This is the problem: man has become a threat to the planet. Multiplied to infinity, serialised in billions, he has lost all sacrality. He has been mass-produced, morphed into a mere digestive system to process products of every kind and, in the end, has become a product himself.'

'Whoever saves one life saves the entire world!? I think I've saved a few, and I know people who've saved a lot, but the world has gone to rack and ruin just the same.'

'All that rampant boorishness, flagrant vulgarity, that cowardice was no longer bearable. It was worse than violence, which at least has a certain grandeur perhaps even in the horror it provokes. Although by then even the violence had become obtuse: arson of what survived of the Mediterranean *maquis*; boulders thrown off motorway bridges, fires in the theatres; attacks on children. It was almost as if beauty, life itself, were the enemy.

I'm not interested in freedom if I have to have breakfast in the bar in the morning rubbing shoulders with this riffraff. Am I bigoted? Maybe I am, perhaps a shred of Leninism has survived within me. When we were young we got worked up about ideas, right or wrong as may be. Recently young people are just angry, full stop: filled with blind hatred that's an end in itself, with the wickedness of lust.'

'Well I personally have absolutely no intention of voting. This system represents the worst nightmares that we could have dreamt of when we were young. I won't have anything to do with it. If I were still young, if I had the energy, I'd be a guerrilla fighter like Lorenzo, Guelfo's brother.'

'No. I will vote. I did last time and I will next time if I'm still around. I can see all the limitations of this system, all the dangers, but we're not living in our times any longer, dear friends. If the 21st century was supposed to be something new, not just another number, well here it is! The explosion of New York shattered the status quo in the most devastating manner, and there's no going back. We have to get used to living in an Empire, without fear. Historically speaking, empires are the form of government that has brought most stability to human society, the greatest welfare and the greatest progress: from the Roman to the Austro-Hungarian Empire. This is a global Empire that takes the decisions necessary at least to avoid catastrophes. The problems are planetary by now, as we all know. And I'm not just talking about economics and production. I'm talking about the survival of the Earth, about trying to save that onion skin that enwraps our home, the Earth: twenty kilometres of fragile atmosphere, by now grievously undermined. Rapid decisions at world level are called for, imposed by force if necessary, as has been done in the last six or seven years. So yes! The Empire, combined with strong, flexible and intelligent local autonomies: that's the path to be followed, the only path. That's why I voted. And the truth is that I'd actually stopped voting under the other system, when my vote counted for nothing. You voted every year and nothing ever changed.'

'Yes, but that may hold for the Western countries who have joined the confederation. Important results have been achieved. Take drugs, for example: now the kids are given a vaccine, like we had polio jabs, and after that they can't take certain drugs. Obviously, we could talk till the cows come home about the ethics of such methods, but they have achieved something. But those who are plundering the world are the hundreds of millions, the billions of wretches trying in any way possible to find the food they need to survive. In the end, you can come to an agreement with the multinationals: you can convince or force them to behave responsibly. But who controls these hordes? Who represents them? These swarms of man-rats, crazed insects who have exterminated the elephants for their tusks, the tigers for their fur, and the gorillas to make ashtrays out of their hands or skulls. People who poison rivers with mercury for a few grams of gold, who burn down a thousand hectares of tropical forest to plant out a potato field. It's more or less the same behaviour that went on in the Western cities before the microchip. They'd kill you to steal a tuppenny-halfpenny watch, to nick your scooter, or simply to pass the time: out of boredom, or sadism.'

'Well, in any case, at least the best have begun to vote again. And we are beginning to see the results of it. People are making better laws, that hold for everyone, even for the 90% who don't vote and have no intention of undertaking the commitments and sacrifices necessary to do so. These laws are changing life for everyone, even for them. They are setting off a virtuous and relentless chain reaction, which will in the end reach the south of the world too, whether it likes it or not. Because the models have always come from the West, even though in the past they were almost always negative.'

'Our civilisation is going through a crisis that is not over yet and we can't know where it's taking us. The twentieth century recorded 170 million deaths, between wars and genocides: a frightful figure. The ideologies on which society has been based since the nineteenth century have for many decades now failed to offer adequate tools to address the great problems of our time. The environment, first and foremost: which doesn't just mean the spread of pollution on planetary scale, but above all the disorientation following on the rupture of the relationship between man's body and soul and between man and nature. It's a crisis of the spirit and of intelligence. The multiplication of consumer goods, generated by a materialist conception of wellbeing and development, has led to an unprecedented moral disorder. And that's just one aspect. There were others, equally serious: for instance, rampant delinquency, the spread of drugs, the lack of respect for old people, the disappearance of the dignity of manual work, the loss of essential virtues such as the sense of personal dignity and the respect for truth. The myth of speed, the tyranny of the image, subjection to instrumental aspects such as personal success and money have caused irreparable damage to the family and the community, to the transmission of the culture and profound identity of our people, of every people. Something had to happen and it has happened, unfortunately. But it's an illusion to think that the problems of individual and collective lack of responsibility can be solved by experts and technology alone, or by stepping up police checks and passing more severe laws. The microchip is a buffer measure to address the emergency. But it can't work on its own. Lofty motivations and civic virtues are called for. We need a plan that will convince individuals and society as a whole of a coexistenceworthy to be called human. In this tempest, our task is to keep hope alive.'

Vincenzo, as usual, had spoken last, summing up the sense, laying down the line to be followed, as he'd been doing for over fifty years. The others, the close friends of a lifetime, listened attentively and in silence. They had always been captivated by him, and respected his intellectual superiority and his charisma. The year before, to celebrate his eightieth birthday, they'd organised an excursion in the Apuan Alps. Guelfo had mobilised his former scout friends to accompany the group of oldsters.

'Guelfo, are you sure? This lot are going to conk out half way up!'

'Don't worry,' replied Guelfo, 'they're tougher than they look.'

And indeed it all went fine, the long walk as far as the Del Freo mountain shelter. Here they had dinner and slept for a few hours; they larked around the whole time, happier than they'd been in a long time. Then the next morning, the ascent to the summit, clambering up, holding onto spurs of rock and taking care not to slip on the clumps of meadow fescue. At the top Guelfo's friends had arranged a sumptuous picnic. Laid out on large white sheets, with bottles of cool Chianti and every conceivable delicacy. There was even a fruit flan with eight big candles. Old age means nothing at all, when the heart still beats so strong...

X

The disease struck suddenly, unexpectedly, like someone who comes knocking at the door in the dead of night. For some weeks Giovanni had been feeling listless and without energy. And so he decided to go to the doctor, a thing he did very rarely, only once every two or three years. They made him do all sorts of tests, and he went to see a couple of specialists. Then, in the surgery of Andrea, a dear friend of his, Giovanni read the fatal answer in his eyes even before he opened his mouth. Andrea gave in immediately to Giovanni's request: he didn't feel like lying. It was cancer, widespread and advanced; there was nothing to be done: it was simply a question of time.

Giovanni was surprised at how calmly he took the news. But then he'd been preparing for this moment for many years. He'd always maintained that preparing to die was a long haul, and the sooner you started on it the better. It had to be faced as soon as you reached the peak of life, when you started on the downhill stretch, but being still so busy and so strong nobody wanted to accept it. But that was the moment when you ought to start, little by little, divesting yourself of your duties and tasks. Now all he was interested in was the time. He wanted to know exactly. Andrea had guaranteed him six months, a year if he reacted well to the treatment. Only now, after all the theorising, did he feel that he had finally succeeded in understanding the secret of time. Time, the passing of which is constantly marked out by rituals, functions, commitments, stimuli, news, needs – real and induced.

Robinson Crusoe sought to remain stubbornly anchored to the time of civilisation with his notches on the wooden post. Giovanni was instead convinced that, in the frenetic world we now live in, we ought to do everything in our power to eliminate these innumerable signs that divide life into empty repetitive segments, within which it's impossible to develop any real project, any true probing of the profound sense of existence. And so - away with the notches! Isolate yourself and sink finally into an unmarked, indeterminate time, stretching into ever-longer moments as we gradually learn to do without, to reduce our needs, to shake off the dross, to scrape off the cultural and material encrustations. Not feeling hunger or thirst, confusing sleep and waking, night and day to finally achieve our possible nirvana. This means giving time back its original dignity as a metaphysical and abstract entity, no longer broken down into hours, days and years but into various states of knowledge and wellbeing in which we can rest and grow until we are ready to give ourselves up to death.

An episode that he had experienced some years before he met Laura kept coming back to his mind. He had recently bought a sailing boat and had set off alone for his holidays. He sailed down as far as the Aeolian islands and anchored in an uninhabited little bay on the southern coast of Lipari. His idea was to spend some time there in total solitude, reading and resting. He had provisions with him, and was completely independent. But then he got a nasty surprise. During the crossing, the sea water had got into his box of stores, which were totally ruined. All that had been saved was a tin of biscuits and a few sachets of sugar. He decided to put off his trip into town for fresh supplies to the next day. But the place was so beautiful, the peace so absolute that he continued to put off this trip. After three days, he wasn't even hungry any more and he went on like this for a week. He hardly even moved the boat, except to change his anchorage depending on the wind. He swam a little, gathered a few sea urchins, read and thought. In the end he stopped reading, and even stopped thinking. The only changes in the days were the alternation of light and darkness.

He slept in the berth, hearing the lapping of the sea on the other side of the thin panel of mahogany. This time they really were the amniotic waters. The waves, the air, the light and the stars passed through his body, finally empty and clean, ready to receive them for the first time. His animal senses, atrophied by two thousand years of culture, of Christianity, of history, began to reawaken, seeking their ancient bonds with the universe. He felt his blood run fast, he became receptive again, ready for a great, free pagan life. In the end, Giovanni found himself living in a state of exaltation which, in his moments of lucidity, even frightened him. He had left a door ajar and gazed onto an unknown chasm that made him feel dizzy. Thinking back, years later, he imagined what the lonely exile in the desert must have felt like for the prophets and the saints. What physical and psychological changes must have taken place in the depths of their being after months, of silence, fasting and solitude.

He had been brought back to life by a little fishing boat, which had come alongside thinking that something had happened, seeing him anchored there for so many days. Speaking to the fishermen was almost like being born again. They gave him some sardines and invited him to dinner in the evening. Giovanni realised that the spell had been broken. He sailed back from the Aeolian islands in one long two-day voyage, carried on the wings of a steady sirocco that swelled the sea and raised the stern in its mighty hand. High in the sky an immense moon sailed in the firmament. He sped past Capri on starboard, Ventotene and his beloved Ponza on port. He never stopped, just as planned. Because the wind wasn't letting up, and it was certainly not going to let him down, so full as he was of creation, so different from when he had left. He'd always regretted that experience, blaming himself for never having managed to repeat it, and for not having taken it through to its ultimate consequences. He'd done something similar a few months after Laura had left him. But it wasn't the same. It had been only an attempt to soothe his pain. But, emptying his body and soul, he had then filled them up even more with her absence and his desire for her.

Giovanni felt himself driven by a strange euphoria. He had left the doctor's surgery almost in a rush, but that had been a gesture of politeness, of concern for his friend who was clearly ill-at-ease. It was almost as if to say: 'That's fine. Don't worry. It's nothing to do with you. Everything's OK. I'll get through, no problem.' Now he walked more slowly, with a hesitant pace, reflecting and letting his thoughts run free. A year was an eternity. Even six months was enough. With death at his side, looking it straight in the eyes, both of them unmasked. This was the ultimate test he'd been waiting for. It was the moment of truth, for him and for everyone: the perfect instant, the final one. He realised that he'd been waiting for it for ever. Since he was young there hadn't been a day of his life that he hadn't thought of death, exorcising it in a thousand different ways, with the kabbalah or obsessive games, like counting steps, the turns of the pedals, the figures on the speedometer. How long will it last with Laura? How many years will I have to see Francesca grow?

Well, now he knew, and this was the way he would have chosen if he could. What he had always been afraid of was an unexpected disaster, an accident, a stupid and unwitting death in a state of total passivity. Of being deprived of that final confrontation, that last opportunity of lifting the veil on life. Giovanni was certain that there was nothing beyond life. He was certain of it in the same way that he believed God was absolutely necessary, to the point of inventing him. And that was indeed what man had done in every epoch, even though since he had begun to base his life on thought, God had had to take a back seat, although it wasn't openly admitted. Only the last two or three generations in the West had believed they could do entirely without God, boasting about it and taking the thrust of the French revolution to its most extreme consequences. They didn't realise that the universal message of 1789 – liberté, egalité, fraternité – not only could sit very comfortably with Christianity, but was actually a direct descendent of it. On the other hand, denying human spirituality was absurd and as transient as the names of the revolutionary months Vendémiaire, Brumiare, or worshipping the supreme deity in the Campus Martius. They'd wanted to see the great bluff that humanity had been handing down through the millennia and the centuries. They'd shown their hands, and those of the deities – but they'd found them all blank, in a suffocating void within which not even a blade of grass could ever grow again.

Giovanni had always lived "as if God existed". He had respected the values, rituals and proprieties which, behind the screen of religion, he knew were the highest forms of coexistence and civilisation that human society had managed to achieve. He had also sought to develop the sentiment of compassion. For years the problems of the people close to him were his problems too. Anyone who approached him received help, understanding and precious advice.

'It's so easy to see into other people's hearts, and obviously it's also part of my work. Frequently we remain imprisoned in cages that we ourselves have made. Like sparrows that, once they get into a house, can't find the open window again, and continue to crash into the ones that are closed until they die, unless someone helps them by showing them the way out. What sort of psychologist would I be if I didn't do that!' For a long time now, and after much mental struggle, he had also realised that goodness is the highest form of intelligence. He had finally grasped what Saint Paul meant in his first letter to the Corinthians when he said that a man could have everything, but if he had not charity then he had nothing. It had been a great enlightenment, because we don't always understand things when we read them, if we're not ready.

The same thing had happened to him when he saw *Three Colours: Blue*, the film by Kiewloski that was part of the *Three Colours Trilogy*: the spiritual testament of the great Polish director who had died many years earlier. In the final sequence, the *Unity of Europe* piece – finally completed by the protagonist, an outstanding performance by Juliette Binoche – accompanies the last images and the credits come up as a soprano sings the words of St. Paul's epistle. Giovanni had remained seated, deeply moved, 'Can it really be that simple?' he wondered, 'so terribly simple and so unattainable?' The usher had called out to him, 'Sir, we're closing'.

As he walked home, he went on thinking about what a precise and direct channel the cinema was. Those characters on the screen made of light, those imagined stories, at times made you feel and engaged you more than similar situations in real life, perhaps because the latter appear with encrustations and superstructures that distance or conceal the emotions, or perhaps because they strike you while you are occupied with other problems. Whereas, sitting there in the dark, we are ready in those two hours to laugh or cry, to feel fear and pain, leaving our own lives outside the door as we buy our ticket. He thought again of Freud, who had elaborated his fundamental theory after having watched a performance of Sophocles' *Oedipus Rex* at the Hofburg-Theater in Vienna, emerging electrified. Talking about this with Vincenzo, his friend had replied: 'Well! What a discovery! Aristotle already said that 2,500 years ago, obviously referring to the theatre and not the cinema.'

When he got home, Giovanni fetched himself a glass of water and sat down in an armchair. The thought passed through his mind that, if he wanted, he could himself have decided how, when and where. The idea that God alone can give and take life is very fine, but it's meaningless. The first hoodlum you come across can shoot you for a pocketful of loose change, any car going along the street can swerve a couple of metres and mow you down because of mechanical failure or the driver's distraction. It's hard to see the hand of God in any of that. And so, why not suicide, why not euthanasia? He remembered having talked about this at length many years before with Giorgio Conciani, a doctor, pianist, gentleman, prophet and ideologist of mercy killing. He was an advocate of death with dignity, to which everyone should be entitled. He had been very struck by that of Arthur Koestler, the author of *Darkness at Noon*. Koestler was very ill; he and his wife had set their house in order, picked up the clothes from the laundry, tidied the cupboards and taken the dog to be put down. Finally they had lain down on the bed and taken their lives. It was all so neat and planned, so terrible.

Giovanni had even fantasised about a Viking funeral. What delusions of grandeur! But it would have been fine, no doubt about it! The boat, with all sails set, the rudder blocked, sailing towards Montecristo in flames. And he himself laid out on the deck. No, no! In the soil, in the cemetery of Trespiano: in the family tomb with all his relatives, waiting for the others. That was his Invalides, his Pantheon. No suicide. He couldn't do it; he would only have considered that if he were losing his marbles. But his brain was working, and the illness wasn't likely to compromise his faculties, at least not right up to the last moments. And so he would bide his time, waiting for destiny to choose the moment. At bottom, at least this element of uncertainty had to be left to chance, that rules over so much of our lives. Taking revenge by stealing the last act from it would not be cricket! His task was to spend well the little time he had left, to draw the most from his miserable capital.

But Giovanni had been in training for this too for some time now. He sought to be selective about his friendships, what he did, what he read. This was interpreted as snobbery, but it wasn't that, or not just that. It was that he knew that we only have a certain amount of time at disposal, and we can't wait to get cancer to realise it. Even before he was fifty he used to say that, counting on a reasonably long life, he would have time to read no more than six/seven hundred books, see about the same number of films, and go to eat out or at friends' houses certainly not more than about one thousand times. Obviously then, all these things had to be carefully chosen and valorised. Frauds and fools had to be avoided like bad wine and vulgar people, books with gaudy covers and titles in big script, houses and objects lacking in elegance. There was nothing decadent or dandy about aestheticism. Giovanni no longer set off to see new places. There would always be a city, a beach, a temple that would have been worth it and that he would never be able to see. When you got to a certain point, what was important was to return to visit the places and the people you already knew. To probe and dig deeper in the places where you had left pieces and traces of your life.

And then there was Francesca. How could he tell her? She usually came back to Florence for a few days every couple of months. By now you could get to Paris by train in less than three hours. He knew that as soon as she found out she would have insisted on staying with him. But Giovanni didn't want that, at least not right away. He wanted to spare her a prolonged torment, and he didn't want her to sacrifice the career she'd just embarked on. Well, he'd find a way round it. On her next visit he'd tell her that he was doing some check-ups and meantime he'd see how the cancer progressed. But it wasn't easy, week after week, bearing this burden without sharing it with anyone. The treatment was beginning to take effect, attacking his body along with the disease. Giovanni felt his vitality decrease; he lost energy and weight. When he shaved in the morning, he wouldn't have been surprised if along with the foam the razor had removed pieces of his face, which he saw wasting away, its contours dissolving, from the increasingly pronounced cheekbones to the long chin.

At least his fate would not hold what is one of the few, sad gifts of old age: solitude, outliving so many other people, living in a world of shadows that you can evoke at will. That sort of borderland between life and death, abandoned by all: even by your own body, by your sight, by your hearing, by your hopes and passions. With the everyday world reduced to a few hesitant repeated gestures, the same little worries: did I switch off the gas? Did I close the front door? The mind, having finally totally mastered existence, being free to sink into the contemplation of memories. And to live all the memories, savouring their purest essence of sensation, the myriad nuances of joy and pain, distilled in memory. Perhaps that's why so many old people appear to be absent. But they're not. It's that they live in another, rarefied world, much more sensitive and lofty than the one they lived in up to a few years before, when they still shared it with others.

Francesca arrived, with the usual gust of energy she brought with her.

'Hi Daddy, I have so many things to tell you. You won't believe it! You know the director of the project... But hey, hang on, you're not well! What's wrong with you?'

'Just the liver, my dear girl. The old liver's been torturing me for weeks.'

'There you are! See what happens if I leave you on your own! All those rich dinners with your friends, and those weird and wonderful sauces you concoct. And then drinking on top of it. Just as I thought. You've overdone it, as usual. What does the doctor say?'

'You know, the usual things. Strict diet and a plethora of pills. One more month and I'll be right as rain.'

'I'll tell Guelfo to keep an eye on you. I can trust him. He's more serious than you!'

That time, they managed to deceive her. Guelfo had sworn on his honour that he would play the part, and he kept his promise. But the next time there was no way of hiding it. The cancer had advanced more quickly than expected, despite the treatment. Giovanni had to tell her the truth. Francesca listened in silence, her eyes glued to her father's haggard face. When he'd finished, she burst out: 'No, no, no! I refuse to accept it. I don't want to. Why didn't you tell me before, you idiot!' It was the first time she'd ever spoken to him like that. 'You've wasted four months,' she went on, 'just thrown them away. But now you're coming to Paris with me. They can do miracles there. And if that's not enough, we'll go to the States. We'll try everything in our power, legal or illegal. We'll buy all the organs you need. There are clinics that do it, I know. I have influential friends at UNESCO, trust me... A new body, if necessary, anything. They take you apart and put you back together again...'

Giovanni put his hands on her shoulders and shook her with the little strength he had left in him. 'Cut it out, Francesca! Stop it, for the love of God! I don't want to hear you saying these things. Everything's fine. I haven't got much pain and I'm well looked after, by friends. I don't want my body turned into a workshop. You know full well what I think about these things. I have my whole life to show for it. And, to tell the truth, I don't have such a strong desire to live at all costs. Perhaps your children will live for two hundred years, and theirs may live for ever. It won't be long now; science is getting there. It'll be a new cataclysm. But I was born in another time, another world. You know that I stood up for this new system. I consider it a necessary evil. But that's a far cry from identifying oneself in what's happening. No, I accept my fate calmly. My time is coming to an end, and that's the way it should be. If it hadn't been for you, my dearest darling, I might have gone even earlier.'

Francesca was lost for words. She was terribly shocked, and there was nothing she could add. It was all so true. She esteemed her father, and respected his intelligence too much to counter with banal arguments. She could have spoken of her own grief, of how the idea that he wouldn't be around tomorrow was unbearable. But that would have meant causing him further suffering, and it would not have been right. The truth was that the year before she'd left for Paris. She'd made her choice and he had encouraged her. It almost seemed as if Giovanni had waited for her to take up her own path with determination before he allowed himself to get sick and die. She got up off the sofa, drying her eyes and sniffing.

'As you wish. But I am going to stay with you to the end, and no discussion! Tomorrow morning I'll go back to Paris and sort out my things, and I'll be back again in the evening. We will share this too … and then, miracles do happen, don't they?'

By now, although he couldn't envisage a particular day, with every day that passed Giovanni felt that the end was approaching. He felt it in the daily reduction of his movements, like a fish in agony swimming in ever-smaller circles. He felt it in the unbearable intensity with which he perceived things, sounds, light, people. It was an obsessive repetition: today I'll do this for the last time, this could be the last. Of course that could be true for everyone, but for me it's different: I know that's the way it is, because in a month I'll very probably be gone.

At times he made it as far as Piazza Signoria, with great difficulty. He remembered that Galileo, blind and dying, had himself taken to that same square so that he could feel his Florence, running his hands over the statues. Even when he was blind, Galileo had intuited the expansion of the universe, while he himself could hardly even sound the depths of his own soul and the results were, in the end, always unsatisfactory. One afternoon he'd decided to return to the Uffizi; it was late and the rooms weren't crowded. It had been a startling experience: the paintings appeared to leave their frames and come towards him. The figures came to life, the Primavera and Venus held out their hands to him. He could hear the clash of pikes on armour in the battle scenes of Paolo Uccello. It was too much. He had sunk down on one of the custodians' chairs and had had to take a taxi home.

Even Francesca's presence often got on his nerves: her concern, and that falsely casual air, the desperate expression that he caught sometimes when she thought he wasn't looking at her. And her unbearable gaze, like that of Medusa. It was as if she were trying to print him indelibly on her memory so that she could keep him always with her. He took Guelfo to one side and begged him to distract her as much as he could, to take her out: in a word, to get her out of his way. Because he could accept his own suffering, but that of Francesca was, quite frankly, too much.

'OK, Giovanni. I'll try, even though she doesn't want to leave your side for a second. But don't be so tragic about it. Francesca and I went to talk to the doctor, and the situation isn't necessarily hopeless.'

'"Don't try to sell me on death, Odysseus", don't you remember that line?' Giovanni replied. 'It speaks for itself, say no more. Ah, wait, there's something else: take this.' And he put into Guelfo's hand the key-ring with the little bronze slave: the keys of the *Gone with the Wind*. 'I leave her to you. I know she's in good hands. There's a bit of work to be done – on the deck, the rigging and so on. I've neglected it a bit in recent years. She too needs young muscles. And, take a word of advice: always sail south. Southwards means sailing towards love.'

Giovanni had left Guelfo standing there stock still – overwhelmed and lost for words – and had gone off to bed, exhausted by all the emotion. Sometimes it seemed to him that he was looking down on himself, stretched out on the bed, that he was looking down on his body, now so fragile, this dry locust's husk, as if he had already left it. It was so hard to remain attached to life. His mind would go off; it would switch off for hours on end, longer every time. Every second was lengthened, suspended in a timeless time, between waking and torpor, in the endless plunge towards death. But life, by now over, held one last ambush for him. One day Francesca told him that she had booked a table in a restaurant:

'Today I want to celebrate, I've had enough of being closed up in here!' Then she helped Giovanni to wash and she dressed him with care. She couldn't help tenderly noticing the way that he brushed his now thin hair. He moved his head closer to the mirror and, for a second, his eyes shone revealing traces of his youth and former roguishness.

'Daddy, there's a surprise for you,' exclaimed Francesca. The door opened and Laura entered the room with her most beautiful smile. Giovanni was so happy he jumped to his feet, finding unknown reserves of energy. 'It must have been the reaction of Alessandro Volta's frog!' he quipped later.

'How long it's been!' said Laura, stretching out her long arms.

'How long indeed,' replied Giovanni. In the evening, when they were alone, he asked her: 'So you've come to give Francesca a hand? You did the right thing. You've saved me a worry.'

'I came for you, Giovanni,' Laura replied. 'For me and for you. This is my place, now. I, who have had so many places, and none of them that was truly mine. If there has been anything real in my life, if it hasn't all been a fairy-tale or a total disaster, my place right now is here. That's what I feel, and that's what I want.'

'No one can deny you that. Your place has always been vacant, waiting for you.'

'I know. I know. What's the point in repeating it. It's something I've told myself so many times over these eleven years… with regret and with shame. But that's the way I am. I'm a mess: I spell trouble for myself and for everyone I meet.'

'Silence! Don't say that, don't say it,' hushed Giovanni, and he got up and started looking through his old LPs. He selected a bolero, and put it on the turntable, not without scratching: *Começaria tudo outra vez, se preciso fosse meu amor. A festa continua, nada foi em vão*. Then he said:

'There the song says it all: I couldn't put it better.'

'You'd really start all over again? So nothing has been in vain… not even the pain?

'Especially that. You're always so beautiful.'

'An old beauty…'

'Not for me, as you well know. Not a day passes that I don't look out the window at the square and see you again with your blue dress and straw hat come from goodness knows where to cheer up the world. For me you will never grow old.'

'Oh Giovanni, Giovanni, you are incorrigible. Adorable and incorrigible! If I had loved myself even a third as much as you loved me, I would have taken more care with my life, I wouldn't have made so many mistakes.'

'You see? Perhaps my destiny was precisely that:

to love you for both of us, to make you understand how precious, unique and unrepeatable you were. To make you happy despite everything, even despite yourself. I think I even managed it for a few years, as long as you allowed me to.'

'You were amazing, a true artist! Of course you made me happy, very happy. And it was a superhuman task, I don't know if you realise how great. Because it's as if I always had a black hole in my soul, a crater that swallowed up everything, everything that was beautiful and good that life offered me over the course of the day. And there was always so much of it, so much; I have been so spoiled! But then the night would take it all away again. As if while I were sleeping my innermost essence, or some evil beast that lived inside me, would systematically destroy everything that I had built during the day. All the precious things, all the love, would suddenly disappear. Like a perverse and bewitched Penelope's cloth. And so every morning I would find myself back at square one, with nothing to show. I was like a modern Sisyphus, having to push my boulder up to the top of the mountain. My God, how awful! Endless times, I simply couldn't find the strength to get up at all, but took refuge beneath the blankets, out of fear, out of despair, making excuses of headaches or menstrual pain. You cured me for over ten years. For every day you would deserve a medal for valour. Then the beast awoke again, more ravenous and more tenacious than ever. To the point of making me leave even Francesca. I feel so ashamed, Giovanni. I'm so pathetic, I make myself sick.'

'Stop it, Laura, please. That's enough. I know all this; Francesca knows it too. We have always understood you. It's pointless to go on torturing yourself like this.'

Laura's arrival shook Giovanni out of the idea of death that he'd by now accepted. For several days he wanted to live with all the energy he had left. He heard her heavy step on the stairs as she returned from shopping, her confident way of moving around the apartment – her home – as if she had never gone away. Indeed Laura had resumed possession without the slightest embarrassment. At that particular moment Rio de Janeiro, her job and her new companion couldn't have been further away. Were Giovanni's illness to continue for several months she would simply remain, in the most natural way possible. Since she belonged to nothing and no-one, it was a luxury she could allow herself. Although she paid a high price for it, because nothing belonged to her and nothing was truly hers, unless it was the love of Giovanni. But even that gave her no pleasure; on the contrary it made her feel even more guilty.

Giovanni had always been struck by the intimacy that women have with death. They know its rhythms and its signals, drawing gestures and tempo from an ancestral memory. It was as if, since they dominate the great magic of birth they had also, to balance it, penetrated the final mystery of death. Not rationally, but in a more profound manner, following the rhythms of the earth, the changing seasons, the movement of the stars. They were priestesses of an infinite ritual, at once ancient and ever new, since the times when their husbands and sons would be borne back to them on their shields. It was this that gave them the strength and the serenity to wash the bodies and perfume and dress them, to purify and put in order the bed and the home, to prepare food and coffee for the relatives and the visitors. And Laura was certain to do the same. His Laura. His? Yes, his. The only man she had had a child with. Laura was perpetuated in Francesca. Her chromosomes went towards the future indissolubly mingled with his.

And suddenly Giovanni realised that this was the task Laura had come for. She was not a messenger of life, but the harbinger of death. She had come to ferry him beyond the last threshold: him, a little man, with all the knowledge and philosophy that were now no use to him at all. A little man who found himself empty-handed and defenceless at the supreme moment. Giovanni felt that it was a privilege to be able to die like this, slowly, surrounded by love in the midst of his own things. Of course it was, but despite that the torment was endless. Torment for the life now irretrievably lost, for not having managed to give it more worth.That was the greatest sin: not having made every moment a moment like this one. He thought again of the death of the Prince of Salina in *The Leopard*, one of his favourite books that he reread regularly, and that had been on his bedside table for years. Except that Giovanni wasn't a prince: he had no titles, palaces or traditions. His things would inevitably be dispersed, his few writings ignored. His only hope was to continue living in Francesca's heart, and perhaps for a little yet in Laura's too. Maybe even in the heart of Guelfo, his last friend, his favourite pupil, the son he had never had. Was it enough? Perhaps not, but what choice was there? The time was up. And so, let it be.

He was propped up against several pillows, but death weighed upon him like an old overcoat. Francesca was lying down next to him, almost as if she was a shield protecting him, contending him with fate up to the last ditch. Laura, sitting on the edge of the bed, held his hand against her cheek.

Suddenly he felt a terrible chill, a cold like he had never experienced before. It started in his legs, which seemed to have turned to marble, and continued to rise up his body. Death was entering into him, taking possession of his body, of what remained of it. He felt an uncontrollable terror and it seemed to him that he let out an agonising cry, although all that emerged was a long groan.

'Daddy, what's wrong?'

'I'm frightened. I'm so frightened and I'm so cold,' he managed to stammer.

In a second Francesca had removed her clothes and climbed into bed beside him, hugging him tight. She clung to him as closely as possible, skin against skin. She held him tight, rocking him gently, humming softly with her mouth resting on his ear, her lips closed. Giovanni relaxed and nodded off. When he opened his eyes again, the light of a late sunset was coming in the window, a pink cloud streaking the clear sky in the distance. Giovanni watched it fixedly, his gaze clear and innocent, purged of all blame, all pain and all debt: the first look of the first man on the dawning of the world. But it lasted only a long, suspended instant. Life, which was leaving him, flooded his heart once again with a huge wave of sweetness. Then it was all over.

EPILOGUE

Guelfo got home around nine and found various messages from Francesca on his answering-machine.

The last one said. 'I called you at one o'clock, at two o'clock and at three o'clock last night and again at seven and at eight this morning. Where the hell are you?'

He called her back: 'Francesca, it's me. What's up? Is everything ok?'

'Everything's fine, perfect. But what about you? Where were you? I've been going crazy trying to get hold of you.'

'You'll never guess. I was at your house; I slept in your bed. It really did me good. No ghosts, no fears. Just that mattress of yours, which has always been so bloody hard!'

There was a silence at the other end. Then Francesca lowered her voice, almost to a whisper. 'But then this must be the night of miracles! Are you sitting down? At seven o'clock last night I found out I'm pregnant. I'm coming home again. Pierre and I arc going to get married in Santo Spirito. My child has to grow up in Florence! Are you happy?'

Now it was Guelfo's turn to be silent for a second. He had left Francesca's house that morning happy, but with the regret that everything it signified had been abandoned and dispersed. Someone, something had heard his prayers. The circle was to be closed and nothing had been in vain. They would go on.

In Francesca's child and those that he too would have, he was now sure of it, there would be the two of them as well as Giovanni, Laura and Lorenzo, something of Michelangelo and Dante, of the Medici and the Lorraine. In that message of harmony between heaven and earth that was Florence's message: the lilies mirroring the stars. A future waiting to be written, on white pages of superb, precious paper that would defy the passage of the centuries.

Postscript

If a second were a million years
And the world as we know it
This wonderful Earth with all its creatures
Existed for a millionth of a second
What a privilege it would have been to have
lived there!
It's something greater than any myth
That in this imponderable void
There could have existed a place like this
And beings like us.

Francis Ford Coppola

When my friend Pagliai of Polistampa proposed to me a new edition of *Paper Heart*, rather than the umpteenth reprint, I willingly agreed. On one condition: that the book should be accompanied by a somewhat sui generis postscript in which I could explain, especially to new readers, what I had in mind when I wrote it almost twenty years ago. Twenty years later! It reminds me of Dumas and the sequel of *The Three Musketeers* or *The Count of Montecristo*. Well, obviously, a lot of things can happen in twenty years: think of the twenty years of Fascism or the last twenty years of Berlusconi now ending in a slow agony. For me twenty years have meant two children, a few more hotels, and the distinct change of perspective that takes place between looking at the world at the age of fifty and moving on to the sixty-eight of today.

Paper Heart is a small book of not much more than 100 pages. I wrote it with what I had to hand, my experiences, my ideas, my memories, the places I loved and the people I met and who shared more or less lengthy pieces of my life. It's a love story. Love for a city as unique as Florence, and the love between various men and women, paced in its different modes and moments. It also talks about politics, religion and art, and I included in it the convictions developed up to the time of its publication. Taking it up again today means reconsidering these opinions, and obviously also assessing whether they have stood the test of time or in what ways they have changed.

I consider myself to be truly privileged. I was born in Florence in 1945, at the end of the war. I have enjoyed sixty-eight years of peace, wellbeing and freedom, conditions that have never existed in Europe for such a long period before. In addition I was also able to experience and savour the last years of a still largely rural culture, since up to 1955 Italy was not very different from what it had been in 1930. My family were respectable people, craftsmen on my mother's side and middle-class on my father's. They were relatively well-off, with sound values that they sought to transmit to me. I have always thought that most of the *fiches* that destiny doles out to you ought to be staked on the stork. Where, when and to whom you are born are variables of such importance that it takes massive efforts and much luck to change them.

Paper Heart begins with an attack on New York in 2014, which happens to be the same year in which this new edition is being published. It's a nuclear attack by Eastern terrorists that causes millions of deaths and totally destroys the city. When the twin towers were destroyed in 2001 many people asked me how I had been able to predict something of this kind. The answer was simple: New York is the nerve centre of the world, the mirror of our civilisation, its most true and symbolic representation. It was logical to assume that if something were to happen it would happen there. It was also easy to understand the attitude of Islamic fundamentalism. A war had to be triggered, a clash of civilisations, otherwise they would have been wiped out in the space of a few decades. Not by missiles or by Western armies, which can't seem to work it out, but by internet, by fashion and music, by so many gadgets and rights – genuine or trumped-up – that characterise our way of life. A way of life that is so easy, comfortable and disenchanted that it is impossible to resist, especially for the new generations and for women, who in so many Muslim countries enjoy very little freedom. The Western model has shattered iron curtains, broken down Chinese walls and the Berlin Wall and swept away ancient traditions like a relentless tsunami. Today it makes us laugh or cry to think of the thirty years of war in Indochina, the endless five-year-plans of the Communist countries that generated misery and death. North Korea is there alone, like an obsessive and deranged concentration camp built around its atomic bomb. The bright lights and skyscrapers of opulent Seoul are just thirty kilometres away, illustrating how capitalism has won everywhere.

My book goes further: the destruction of New York brings about a new world order. "Along with the Rockefeller Center and the Moma, the Metropolitan and the Plaza, a hundred years of dialectic had gone up in smoke. All that remained of the eternal debate of Western civilisation between individual freedom and the need for State control was turned to ashes." It's not like that yet. We don't have the implanted microchip for identification. But already over half the crimes are detected with the help of the closed-circuit TVs that watch over our streets, or the mobile phones that record our movements and our conversations. Iris recognition is by now routine in the States, and technology can reveal traces of our movements even decades later. It's only a question of time before such controls become increasingly more widespread and effective. And in a society that is ever more chaotic, violent and multiethnic, I don't see how we can do without them. This is why my hope was for new forms of democracy, more selective and loftier. It shouldn't be taboo to speak about a system where the right to vote is sought and earned. Suffice it to look at what has been happening in our country for so long now: "The last popular elections had been held in Italy in 2013, but by that stage there were elections every year and practically nothing ever changed. The governments were increasingly conditioned by contingencies, terrorised by the daily opinion polls that attributed votes to every single prime ministerial or ministerial move, so that it was impossible to implement a genuine policy of wide-ranging reform."

Now that we're there, we could say that things are even worse than what I predicted. I've always been fascinated by politics; I think that putting yourself at the service of your city, your country, other people is the finest and most noble activity that any citizen can aspire to. Even the comment of Pope Bergoglio, who came from Argentina and now lives in Italy, made a bit of a stir, when he referred to two countries brought to their knees by the appalling management of the institutions. In Italy the real drama was paralysis, when politics was reduced to an ideological clash, to tactics, to ambush. An endless chess game where no-one ever won and Italy always lost. Political and entrepreneurial talent has been lacking for too long. The only one we have is Marchionne, currently CEO of Fiat-Chrysler: the results speak for themselves and that's why he's so hated. Renzi, whom I've known since he was a lad, certainly has what it takes, the charisma and the determination. Now he's Prime Minister, but the reforms he's trying to introduce come up against potent resistance from the bureaucratic system. But this doesn't mean that we have to abandon a noble idea of politics.

Since I was young I have admired Prezzolini, Walter Lippman and Montanelli for their clarity and seriousness and the way they shun facile utopias. At heart, my position has never really changed, despite indulging in detours. I viewed the student protests of 1968 with a mixture of irritation and suspicion. People in Italy had never had it as good as in the 1960s, and it was incomprehensible for me to see the intelligentsia marching with Chairman Mao's *Little Red Book* in their hands. Over the last thirty-five years I've spent half my time holding the most varied positions all over Florence, always offering my services free of charge. I militated in the Radicals, I founded the Green party, the *Verdi*, in Tuscany with a group of friends. Giovanni's friends in the book are my friends: smart people who've never let me down, a true aristocracy. "Actually the definition of aristocracy is spot-on. It has nothing to do with blood or birth. The true aristocrats are those who possess strength and greatness of soul, the capacity for solitude, combined with profound goodness and a total lack of self-interest."

Friendship is a very important thing, which can be eternal and at the same time extremely fragile. In the book I wanted to recall those friends of mine who had died: Eugenio Banzi, Guido De Masi, Giorgio Conciani, Sandro Steiner, Mauro Buffi. Sadly, since I wrote the book they have been joined by many others, whom it would now be impossible to recall. I have had many friends of every type and kind. The friends of my youth were particularly turbulent, companions of one-off escapades. I even had to go and collect a couple of them when they were let out of prison or the criminal asylum, and in some way I helped them to get back on their feet. I believe that, in the end, character is our destiny, and that it can be only partially changed.

The book is set in Florence, the anchorage of my life, and partly in Rio de Janeiro, where my father grew up, where my grandparents are buried and where a large part of my family lives. I myself lived there for five years, and I always return with pleasure. They are two cities that are very different and both magnificent. Every day I cycle round Florence (the bicycle being the only vehicle I use), and it is my greatest privilege. I always discover something new – a detail that had escaped me – you can never find out all there is to know about this city. What great good fortune to have been born and lived here! Camus, gazing over Florence from the Boboli hill defined it as "a cry of stone, where the theories of Plotinus and Nietzsche meet and allow man one last hope".

Anyone who wants to understand the soul of Florence has to start from the Baptistery, from its Platonic and Proto-Christian geometry, the seat of an eternal God whose power radiates throughout the city. Opposite it Brunelleschi's Cupola is so huge it could easily contain the Baptistery, the way a concrete bell envelops the nucleus of an atomic power station, ensuring that its infinite energy is released little by little to meet human requirements. To simplify, we could say that the Baptistery – an ancient Roman temple dedicated to Mars – encloses the God of the Bible, God the Creator, who inflicts all sorts of sufferings on Job and when Job protests replies contemptuously: "Where wast thou when I laid the foundations of the earth?" Santa Maria del Fiore is the God of the Gospels, Christ who saves the world with his mercy and his infinite charity, born from Mary's pregnant womb, the Cupola, which contains all the Florentines and – symbolically – all humanity. 2012 marked another outstanding moment in the two-thousand-year life of the Baptistery, when during the 10 days of the Florens event it was transformed into a new Golgotha. The crucifixes of Brunelleschi, Donatello and Michelangelo were set up one next to the other to create a new crucifixion scene where the thieves too became Christ. And what is that, if not the true Resurrection? I went to see it every day, notwithstanding the long queues, dragging my friends along. I begged the president of Florens, Giovanni Gentile, to have the event prolonged, but it was impossible for bureaucratic reasons, and also for motives of security and insurance. I was very disappointed, but then I realised that this "miracle" was a genuine exception and had to remain such.

The apartment of Giovanni and Francesca in Piazza Santo Spirito is my apartment. We had to leave it on account of the stairs, but we didn't sell it. It's being rented and waiting there for when my children, Corso and Verdiana, one day want to fill it with their lives. Now we live in Piazza D'Azeglio, which is very different but equally beautiful and in the book is Guelfo's district. Everything takes place in the old centre of this city. For the figure of Giovanni I drew inspiration from my analyst, Carlo Poggiali, who also died a few years ago. We are now editing a collection of his poems, the last gift he left us.

The *Gone with the Wind* was my first sailing boat, later replaced by the *Leopoldo*, an old wooden motorsailer which last year I gave as a present to Niccolò, a lad that I've known since birth, the son of dear friends of mine. A gift made not on account of illness, as in the book, but simply because I hardly ever used it and it needed youthful strength and enthusiasm. As I said at the start, *Paper Heart* is a home-made work fabricated from everyday materials.

At this point I feel duty bound to tell you about the "discoveries" I have made over the last few years, which at this stage I believe are fairly definitive. In 2000 I began to return to the fold, to a faith that I had practised as a child and a boy, and that I then abandoned in my youth and never sought again. In fact, in the book I defined Giovanni as "brilliantly atheist". That's something I wouldn't do now, but even then I ought to have defined him as "a devout atheist". The book also expresses a declared admiration for Pope Wojtyla, and confirms the importance of religion as the basis for every society. It is a fact that all the Popes that I have seen elected in the course of my existence have been of the highest calibre: Roncalli, Montini,

Wojtyla, Ratzinger, Bergoglio, and the very brief papacy of Pope Luciani. And there was always an alternation between a more innovative Pontiff and a more traditionalist one, in a perfect equilibrium in which those who believe see the hand of the Holy Spirit. The others cannot fail to see the wisdom of a millennial institution. It would be as if Italy had been governed by six De Gasperis in a row, instead of the ongoing disaster that we have brought down upon ourselves. And we really did go on pilgrimage to Rome in 2000 for the Jubilee, along the Via Francigena, as predicted in the book, but without the donkeys and carrying the rucksacks on our backs. It was a fundamental experience for many of us. Some even did the pilgrimage to Santiago de Compostela. So far I haven't had the thirty-five or forty days necessary, so I'm keeping it in reserve as a seventieth birthday present.

In any case, God had not forgotten me and he came to look for me, initially through the person of Father Gino Ciolini, the prior of Santo Spirito, an Augustinian and a fine philosopher. We became acquainted at his conferences, which continued a centuries-old tradition; they were often attended by Massimo Cacciari, a famous philosopher and mayor of Venice for ten years. Father Ciolini had reawakened me, he had grasped my attention, and the effect was to put me back on track. God did the rest, through two unequivocal episodes. One took place in the Church of the Holy Sepulchre in Jerusalem and the other in the church of Bolsena. When I told Father Ciolini about them, he replied: "Riccardo I have been in this convent for sixty years, studying and praying all day long. Only four or five times have I been able to lift the veil on reality in a way similar to what you describe. And it has happened to you twice in just a few months. Count yourself lucky and thank the Lord."

I know that now in the West, especially in pseudo-intellectual bourgeois circles, faith is out of fashion, especially the Catholic faith. It's just about ok if some-one becomes a Buddhist – certainly trendier – where-as being Catholic is definitely not the thing. Well, this is what I say to you: like me you know nothing about quantum physics or string theory, you don't even know anything about the technology that makes your mo-bile phone work. Increasingly we stop at the surface of things, at mere appearances and that's sufficient for us. But sometimes all it takes is a newspaper article, a book happened on by chance, a TV programme late in the evening that we linger to watch without chang-ing channel, and a whole hitherto unknown world can open up before us. Well, dear friends, don't change channel when the notion of God crosses your mind for an instant, perhaps when you happen to be in church for a wedding or a funeral, or when you're bringing flowers to the cemetery. God is like a beggar; he will come knocking at your door and if you don't open, he'll come back again and again. And then one day he won't come back, and that's when things really get difficult.

I am now certain that there is life after death. I am not capable of explaining where this certainty comes from, but it is a voice that I hear clearly in my heart and soul. Of course, there are days when faith wavers, and everything returns to being ephemeral and mean-ingless. Even Saint Augustine was suspicious of those who never had doubts; he said that faith had to be lost and regained every day. Finally, I would urge you to go at least once to Jerusalem. I returned in 2012, on pilgrimage with the Franciscan friars who have been custodians of the holy places since 1200, and it was more wonderful than ever. Jerusalem is unique and magical, the spiritual centre of the world, and one day I hope that I can go and live there for a while. I feel that no-one ought to end their life without having med-itated at length and calmly on the great mystery with-in us, on those last questions that have always ac-companied man's journey

I have lived surrounded by beauty, and I have sought it incessantly and in an entirely spontaneous manner. I read somewhere that beauty is the dress of goodness, like a promise of happiness. The intuition is that, if there is beauty there is good too, there must be something great. In Florence, at times the intensity of beauty is unbearable. When I was a boy I played ball in front of Santa Maria Novella, in front of Alberti's facade; if you did it now you might even be arrested. This familiarity with the art and harmony of Florence has been a good school. I have learnt to recognise it in its multiple forms, and gradually to remove all the trumpery surrounding it that makes it cheap. I have always frequented museums, churches and ancient cemeteries. Sometimes I am very hurried and I skip what I'm not interested in, especially in a gallery. Being accustomed to a place like the Uffizi makes you selective. In *Paper Heart*, speaking of the twentieth century I comment very critically, "Small wonder then that great art abandoned it before it was even half-way through". This is a judgement that I have reflected on at length. Today, I still think that it is true, especially for painting, sculpture and music. Some time ago I found small book written by Bernard Berenson in 1950. A wonderful little essay called *Piero Della Francesca or The Ineloquent in Art*, where in just a few pages he expresses his opinion on the known art of the world. The best thing I can do is to quote it, since I do not think it can possibly be better expressed. One can only imagine what Berenson would have thought had he been able to view the rampant avalanche of installations and dark rooms, of which the Venice Biennale is the sacrilegious temple!

...the kind of art (in all fields) which has hitherto been regarded as normal, except for such periods as the eclipse of culture that in the Latin world lasted from about 500 to 1100 of our era. This art,

to which society kept returning after every temporary aberration, every momentary whim, every cow-
boy incursion, every High-Church nihilism, has been
called "classical".

I adhere to the canons of classical art with pride
as well as conviction, and maintain that where its
standards were upheld there was no room for "ex-
pressionism". Indeed, I go further and defy the art-
historians to show me a great masterpiece of the last
fifty centuries where the expression is inflated – I
mean beyond the requirements of the action, and
this action in turn more vehement, more violent than
the subject demands. I dare assert that for me, the
less expressive a statue or painting, and the more it
makes me feel its existence, its full existence, the
more life-enhancing do I find it, as so perfectly ex-
emplified by the figures of Piero della Francesca.
[...]

So we may permit ourselves to generalize about
this art of the past, and to affirm that in moments
hitherto almost universally esteemed greatest, it has
always been as ineloquent as Piero della Francesca
himself, as mute and as glorious. I am tempted to
go further and suggest that perhaps real art in the
visual realm (as distinct from no matter what in-
formation, what mere newness, what drolleries,
what jokes) always tends to communicate the pure
existence of the figure presented.

Real art never has nor should represent, but
present. Art is based on actuality, but exists inde-
pendently, without looking to the spring-board from
which it launches itself into the ocean of Itness. Real art is It, and with the Jehovah of the Old Testament should answer, as he when asked Who He was,
"I am that I am." (*)

_____

(*) Biblioteca Berenson, Villa I Tatti – The Harvard University
Center for Italian Renaissance Studies, courtesy of the President
and Fellows of Harvard College

Let me now cite another author:

> The future is undiscernible because it has not
> yet come into existence; its potentialities are infi-
> nite, and therefore the future cannot be predicted
> by extrapolating from the past. [...] there is no prece-
> dent for the power that Man has acquired over the
> biosphere in the course of the two centuries 1763 –
> 1973. In these bewildering circumstances, only one
> prediction can be made with certainty. Man, the
> child of Mother Earth, would not be able to survive
> the crime of matricide if he were to commit it. The
> penalty for this would be self-annihilation. [...]
> Will mankind murder Mother Earth or will he
> redeem her? He could murder her by misusing his
> increasing technological potency. Alternatively he
> could redeem her by overcoming the suicidal, ag-
> gressive greed that, in all living creatures, including
> Man himself, has been the price of the Great Moth-
> er's gift of life. This is the enigmatic question which
> now confronts Man.

This extract is from *Mankind and Mother Earth* by
Arnold Toynbee, the greatest historian of the twentieth century, a work dating to 1976 – possibly the last,
almost a testament. So many things have changed over
the last forty years, all too often for the worse, and human greed and aggressiveness appear, if possible, to
be more blatant than ever. At the same time there has
also been enormous progress in all fields of science,
medicine in particular. The amazing experiments carried out at the CERN in Geneva have brought us back
to the precise moment of the Big Bang from which the
universe originated. We're riding a wave that we can't
stop and we can't get off. We are an arrow shot towards infinity and it's absurd to think that we will set
ourselves limits, at least in scientific research. I don't
know how it will all end up; no-one can know. But, despite everything, I have faith in our destiny. If we are

made in God's image, then we will pursue our path right to the end. We will colonise the universe, bringing with us Shakespeare and Dante, Michelangelo and Mozart. The path is a narrow one: on one side there's Icarus and on the other Lucifer. We're in the middle, with our virtues, our knowledge, our ethics and our courage as our only compass. And love, yes: love. We will fill this empty and silent cosmos with love. How I'd love to live to see that!

Having said that, don't be misled into thinking that I've become an ardent disciple of technology, or that I have yielded to the breeze that blows and whispers: "Everything, is possible, everything is allowed". *Paper Heart* was a manifesto in favour of the printed page against the invasion of the computer, the web and virtual reality. I myself don't have a computer, which I wouldn't know how to use anyway. A few years back I had to give in to the mobile phone, and only recently I've learnt how to send text messages. I still write lots of letters by hand in lovely blue ink and I find life wonderful. Being a Christian I feel compassion for those who read books on tablets, and I wouldn't give up my library for anything in the world. I live surrounded by books which I unsuccessfully attempt to keep in order. My love of literature has increased greatly in recent years. I think that, even when we are old and ailing, as long as we can read life retains much of its value. I have made many discoveries in this period: James Hillman, Roger Scruton, Cormac McCarthy and Vasilij Grossman to mention just a few of those who have struck me most. I adore the cinema and I think that a good film should be seen in the dark in the movie theatre, all together, as a collective ritual. As it turned out, a few years ago I became president of France Odeon, the Florence festival of French cinema. This allowed me to get to know this world from inside, and to gorge myself on films from all over the world at Cannes.

I believe in the culture of the limit: the limit of good sense in individual behaviour. I favour duties over rights, which have spiralled out of control in recent years. I continue to believe that the cornerstone of society is the union between a man and a woman, who preferably give birth to children. In this way they assume responsibility and learn the lessons of sacrifice and disinterested love that a child inevitably teaches. This is why I am against homosexual marriage, while obviously guaranteeing all civil rights to couples who choose to live together. However, allowing such couples to adopt children, who are thus prevented from uttering the words "mummy" or "daddy", seems to me the height of folly and not even worth wasting one's breath on. It would appear that the parliaments of Western countries think differently, giving in to these claims one after another. Since they are no longer able to promise everything to everyone, they have opted for the easier course of "permitting everything to everyone" through to the ultimate aberration of the European Union, with its new documents where the words "Mother" and "Father" have been replaced with "Parent 1" and "Parent 2". If only for this reason I would stick with the Catholic Church, which alone has defended man's dignity and good commonsense. I believe in a natural law that is innate in every human being, together with the concept of good and evil, a law that cannot be changed at will to fit with passing trends. That's why I can't stand the conformist mawkish amalgam of the politically correct: spawned by two cultures – lay and Marxist – that couldn't fit together except on the weakest and most superficial issues. As T.S. Eliot said: "They constantly try to escape/From the darkness outside and within/By dreaming of systems so perfect that no one will need to be good." If we continue along this path our decadence will be relentless. Other great civilisations have already been through it, wiped out by other civilisations that were undoubtedly cruder but perhaps for this very reason stronger and more cohesive, ready to take our place.

Who know, perhaps I am simply a conservative who has taken to heart Pasolini's admonition: "defend, preserve, pray". But since I am passionate about history I feel that I am capable of judging human events with a certain lucidity. When I read Thucydides' *The History of the Peloponnesian War* at the age of seventeen, it was a revelation. Athens, a naval power devoted to global trade pitted against a power that was unbeatable on dry land, Sparta. An identical schema is to be found in the wars of England against France, Spain and, finally, Germany. Right up to the conflict between the United States and Russia.

I love life, I love it enormously, and the words that I quoted at the start of this postscript written by Francis Ford Coppola– with whom I shared an almighty booze-up in a long-ago night in Rio de Janeiro – perfectly express my own feelings. I could extol a hymn to joy that would take up an entire book. Every time I see the sea I am moved, when I can set off on foot with a knapsack on my back I am perfectly happy and my heart returns to that youth which in truth I have never really left behind, which is my real home. Perhaps the art of withstanding time is being able to age without ever becoming entirely adult: this allows us to reach the end intact.

My splendid Lucia: my wife, to whom I dedicated this book in 1997 and who partly inspired the character of Francesca, continues to be splendid. She is so much better than I am that she forces me to a breathless pursuit in the vain hope of even trying to keep up with her. She's the happiest person I know. Perhaps it's because she has never concerned herself with Good – in the sense of the great, abstract absolute in the

name of which such immense disasters have been per-
petrated. She has instead settled for a humble and
spontaneous Goodness towards anyone or anything
that crosses her path, be they people, animals or plants.
Every so often I reproach her – otherwise what are husbands for? – forher lack of interest in travelling, where-
as I am a born traveller. Then one night, in a hospital
car park, fresh from a particularly sad visit, she said
to me: "You see, I can't go away for more than a few
days. My little world – that I've built with so much effort – would suffer, and I'm afraid that when I come
back I might not even find it again. I have to attend to
the fire, to make sure it never goes out."

Naturally the idea of death, which is such a strong
presence in *Paper Heart*, has not receded with the passage of time. But I have learned to accept it, obviously more for myself than for the people I love. Every so
often the magnificent line from Baudelaire's "Le Voyage" comes to mind: "Ô Mort, vieux capitaine, il est
temps! levons l'ancre!" I should like to leave you with
an extract from the poem "Goodbye and Best Wishes"
by Pasolini, which has already been used by Camillo
Langone in his fine book *Manifesto della Destra divina*,
but I'm sure he won't mind. I think it very beautiful, a
fitting testament to the most important Italian intellectual of the post-war period. It was translated from
the Friuli dialect into Italian by the poet himself.

> Well, boy in a dead man's socks,
> I've told you what they want of you, the Gods
> of the fields. There, where you were born
> Where as a child you learned
> their Commandments. But in the City?
> There, not even Christ is enough.
> It takes the Church: but it has to be
> modern. And it takes the poor.
> As for you, defend, preserve, pray:
> but love the poor, love their difference.

Love their desire to live alone
in their world, amidst meadows and buildings
where word of our world
does not reach; love the boundary
they've drawn between us and them;
love the dialect they invent each morning,
so no-one understands, so they don't have
to share their joy with anyone.
Love the sun in the city and the poverty of the
thieves, love the flesh of the mother in the son.
Inside our world, don't say
you're a bourgeois, but that you're a saint
or a soldier: a saint without ignorance,
or a soldier without violence.
Bear in your saint's or soldier's hands
your closeness to the King, the divine
Right that is within us, in sleep.
Believe in the blind honesty of the bourgeois,
even if it's an illusion; because
even the masters have their masters,
and are sons of fathers
who are somewhere in the world.
It's enough that the mere feeling
of life should be the same for all:
the rest doesn't matter, youth holding
the Book without the Word in your hand
Hic desinit cantus. You take
This burden upon your shoulders.
I cannot: no-one would understand
the scandal. An old man respects
the judgement of the world: even
if he cares nothing for it. And he respects
what he is in the world. He must
protect his weakened nerves,
and play the game he has never played.
You take this weight, boy who hates me,
you carry it. It will shine in your heart. And I
shall walk lightly, moving forward, choosing always
life, youth.

INDEX

PRINTED IN FLORENCE
AT THE TIPOGRAFIA EDITRICE POLISTAMPA
IN THE MONTH OF JULY 2015